WARNING!

VAMPIRES
are
LiVing
next
Door!

Look out for Dinah's other hilarious books:

WARNING!
ALIENS are Invading the School!

WARNING!
COMPUTERS are Eating my Friend!

WARNING!

VAMPIRES are LiVing next Door!

Dinah Capparucci

SCHOLASTIC

First published in the UK in 2010 by Scholastic Children's Books
An imprint of Scholastic Ltd
Euston House, 24 Eversholt Street
London, NW1 1DB, UK
Registered office: Westfield Road, Southam, Warwickshire, CV47 0RA
SCHOLASTIC and associated logos are trademarks and/or registered
trademarks of Scholastic Inc.

Text copyright © Dinah Capparucci, 2010

The right of Dinah Capparucci to be identified as the author
of this work has been asserted by her.

Cover illustration © Fred Blunt, 2010

ISBN 978 1 407 11209 1

A CIP catalogue record for this book is available
from the British Library.

Printed by CPI Bookmarque, Croydon, CR0 4TD
Papers used by Scholastic Children's Books are made from
wood grown in sustainable forests.

1 3 5 7 9 10 8 6 4 2

www.scholastic.co.uk/zone

To my brilliant Leon and Maisy.

With many thanks to Moose (who wishes his pedigree and affiliations to remain anonymous) for sharing his extensive knowledge of fireworks with me.

The Fireworks Code

- You have to be eighteen years old before you are allowed to buy fireworks in the shops. Never play with fireworks. They are dangerous and can hurt you.
- Only adults should light and hold fireworks.
- Never go near a firework when it has been lit. Even if it hasn't gone off, it could still explode.
- When you are watching fireworks, always stand well back.
- If you are given a sparkler, always wear gloves. Always hold sparklers at arm's length.
- When a sparkler goes out, DON'T TOUCH IT. It could still burn you, so put it in a bucket of water, hot end down.
- Never give sparklers to a child under five.
- Fireworks will scare your pets, so keep them safely indoors.

One

My name is Jordan and my mate's name is Boy Dave because his dad is Big Dave. I should say at this point that none of this was our fault. There were a few problems with some larger than life-sized reindeer and the vampires next door. I think it was the hens that were the final straw, but really there were quite a few things in our little box of phobias and it could have been any of them.

Basically there was a lot of black smoke and quite a few people got way too hysterical for the situation. As usual we got blamed for everything, although our other mate Ryan didn't get as much of the blame as we did.

Anyway, coming back to the beginning, I suppose the story really began in October, a few days before Halloween, on a Thursday afternoon.

It was four o'clock on one of those orange-brown October days. The pathways in the woods behind us were thick with fallen leaves, and the sun, which had been watery white for most of the day, was going down in quite a nice orange blur. From my, Boy

Dave's and Ryan's points of view all this nice mild weather was a bit depressing.

We were crouched at the edge of an open-air swimming pool behind the Old Manor house. It was part of an old sports area. There was a tennis court with a drooping net, and across a courtyard on the opposite side of the pool were some falling down stables. For as long as we could remember the pool had been a spider pit full of rubble, but last year the Old Manor was turned into a hotel and it became a proper pool again.

The bad news was it was only for the hotel guests.

Obviously we tried to bunk in a few times but they held parties on the courtyard almost every night, so in the end we more or less gave up. Now, though, it was different. The pool had been emptied for winter and the place was deserted. Which was just as well. We were busy making a winter activity of our own and preferred not to be disturbed.

"The temperature today is eight point five degrees Celsius," said Ryan, who is into science normally, but seemed to be particularly (and rather boringly) into winter science this year. "It's possible we'll hit zero over the next month or so."

"If it isn't going to happen for a month," said Boy Dave, eyeing the old hose that was drooping pathetically over the edge, "I don't see why we have to do it now."

"If we wait until it's actually freezing," said Ryan, a bit irritably (we were all getting to that ratty stage of boredom and being cold), "the pipes might freeze too, and then the tap won't work."

I lifted the tarpaulin and peered into the spidery darkness underneath. "It doesn't seem to be working very well now."

For a moment we all squinted through the gloom to the puddle at the bottom of the pool. It didn't look like it had got any bigger since the last time we'd checked.

We listened in depressed silence to the dismal sound of the hose trickling for a bit, then Ryan said, "Well you can't expect it to be like filling a bath."

His voice echoed eerily against the pool walls. "I'd say that must be a volume of . . . oh . . . thirty-two metres cubed."

"Well I dunno about anyone else –" I rubbed my hands together, trying to get back the circulation "– but I'm getting really hungry. I reckon the best thing to do would be to go home now and come back in the morning. I mean –" I tried to sound positive "– it's not as if there's any risk of it overflowing."

"Do you think we'll need to get ice skates?" I asked as we jumped down the other side of the wall and headed back into the woods.

"Nah, we can just slide about on our shoes. Or even. . ." Boy Dave looked excited for the first time in two hours. "Get our skateboards and do, like, extreme sports."

"I could probably invent some really good extreme sports," said Ryan, "that no one's ever heard of before."

We gave him a bit of a look.

"Bearing in mind that we don't want to actually die during them," said Boy Dave. "You know, just to get that straight quite early on."

Ryan blinked at him through his glasses. "There has to be a good chance you'll die. Or they wouldn't be extreme."

"Well. . ." I tried to be tactful. "Maybe you could just do some quite exciting sports where there's a possibility of us having a bit of an accident, but one which we would most likely survive?"

Ryan, who (now I thought about it) had been even more irritable than usual lately, glared at me.

"Inventing things isn't as easy as everyone seems to think. I mean, people say, 'Oh you could invent this, or that' and then think I can just go off and do it." He sniffed. "It can be a very lonely process."

Me and Boy Dave looked at each other. With Ryan's ideas being what they were, we weren't totally convinced about the people encouraging him bit. On the other hand, this invention, whatever it was, seemed to have really got to him.

"Erm," I asked timidly, "are you . . . I mean, is there by any chance a particular. . ."

"That's not going very well?" finished Boy Dave.

Ryan kicked at a pile of leaves. They flew into the air in an angry flurry.

"It's very tricky! Very tricky! Inventing things doesn't happen just like that! It requires a great deal of research and experimentation."

"We've got invention problems too, you know," Boy Dave told him. "Like inventing a way of getting sixty quid by Christmas."

I suppose Ryan's worries had reminded him of our own. I wished they hadn't, though.

It was like this: Mine and Boy Dave's parents had decided that now we were twelve we ought to buy our own Christmas presents. I don't mean just choose them. I mean actually pay for them.

Our dads must have been colluding big time because when we howled, "Don't be ridiculous – all those relatives? On our meagre pocket money? When we don't even like them?" They both miraculously (in separate houses, but at more or less the same time) thought of a "solution".

"Hmm." (This is our dads looking around wonderingly.) "Oh! What a coincidence, two really messy leafy gardens with twigs and mud and stuff. I might just have the answer! You can clean up the garden and I'll give you thirty quid. That way you'll be able to buy your own Christmas presents after all. Hooray! Superdad saves the day."

Obviously what had really happened was our mums had moaned and moaned about the messy gardens for weeks and our dads had hatched a plot to pass the job on to us.

Luckily, by the time we'd managed to trek mud through our houses a few times, our mums were giving our dads "just give them their money and do it yourselves" type looks, so in a way it worked out quite well.

Unfortunately, all this happened a bit too ahead of Christmas, if you catch my drift.

"OK," I sighed. "How many days is it until Christmas again?"

Ryan did a quick calculation. "Sixty."

We walked on for a bit in silence.

"And how much did you say you had left?" I asked Boy Dave eventually.

"Seventy-five pence. You?"

"Mine's a bit better. One pound, thirteen."

There was another silence while we imagined Christmas day – when we didn't actually have any presents to give anyone. The embarrassment would be bad. But our dads wanting to know what we'd done with their money would be worse.

The trouble was we didn't really know. There had been a few trips to the seaside, some burgers and chips, a couple of bars of chocolate. Then there were the cool "must have" T-shirts; other little things here and there.

"I did have an idea about that." Ryan seemed to have cheered up a bit. He likes finding solutions. Also, maybe he'd realized that compared with our huge problems one of his inventions not going very well wasn't the end of the world.

I should explain that Ryan doesn't have the same Christmas worries as us. His mum's an artist (is what she likes to call it) and believes that not making your own Christmas presents is commercial and terrible. And Ryan doesn't even mind making his own presents. In that way his problem was kind of the opposite to ours. One batch of his last year's gifts had the side effect of messing up radio waves and his relatives had to spend Christmas day without TV, radio and mobile phones. And the microwave went completely unprogrammable so whenever they put something inside it there was no way of knowing what it was going to do.

The other batch blew up the Christmas tree before they were even opened.

It had got to the point where even if Ryan tried to give someone a Christmas present, they wouldn't take it.

"Right," said Ryan. "So, we need to get sixty quid in sixty days. A pound a day in other words."

"Well we probably need a couple of days to actually buy them as well," I told him sensibly.

"I hate choosing presents," said Boy Dave.

"The way things are going," I said gloomily, "we'll be making them, never mind choosing them. Not complicated stuff," I said hastily, seeing the look he shot me. "I mean, like, maybe a batch of washing-up liquid bubble bath. I made some for my sister's birthday and she must have thought it was real because she never said anything."

Boy Dave sighed. "Then again, if we still had the money we could just buy it. And I could probably handle choosing that."

I was just about to point out that bubble bath comes in all different shapes and sizes when Ryan coughed and pushed his glasses up his nose in a particular way.

"Actually, I've invented something that could make us a great deal of money. Initial tests have been very successful and I think I can safely say, we are now in a position to charge quite large sums to witness them in action."

He waited expectantly.

"Well, go on then," I said tiredly. Given that Ryan's inventions normally end up having the opposite effect to making us money we weren't too excited.

"The most spectacular fireworks ever invented," he announced grandly. "Next year I hope to go into mass production, but unfortunately this year, time-wise, I have only been able to perfect three."

"Three?" we echoed.

"I don't mean those pathetic sparkly little things that are over in a few minutes," said Ryan snootily. "Mine are a completely unique, new type of firework. Just one of them is spectacular. Three together is positively an . . ." he searched for the word, ". . . *extravaganza!*"

There was a bit of a silence.

"And on a scale of one to ten," asked Boy Dave, "what are the chances of us being blown to bits?"

"Seven?" Ryan considered. "No, probably more like four. I mean, they're pretty safe. Safer than most other sorts in a way, especially with the proper safety procedures in place."

"And you're sure we're not talking extreme fireworks here?" I asked worriedly.

"Extreme-ish." Ryan looked cagey. "The point is, do you want to earn back your fifty-eight pounds, twelve pence or don't you?"

It's one of those things about friendship. Basically it's about believing that, no matter how much it might seem like it, your friend probably hasn't decided to kill you. And four wasn't a bad score. At least it was the right side of five.

Two

Almost as soon as I got home I could tell things weren't right. For a start there was no smell of any food being cooked. Considering how hungry I was this was especially obvious.

When I went into the living room my great Auntie Dulcie was sitting at the table feebly polishing some large silver knives and forks. She gave me one of her "if I had known it was going to be like this, I would have gone to live in Sunset Villas" looks, but I wasn't really paying attention.

The rest of the room was in chaos. All the furniture was pulled away from the wall and Mum, who looked like some sort of inmate on day release, was busy vacuuming the bits of carpet that no one ever sees. The biggest shock of all, though, was my dad. He appeared to be – I goggled – dusting.

"Um hell-oo," I cleared my throat politely, "any chance of getting something to eat around here?"

I mean, I wasn't exactly expecting Mum to go, "Certainly, darling, you know I live to serve you," but the unleashing of the thousand howling devil-beasts from her mouth was somewhat unexpected. Under fire from this completely unnecessary abuse I backed towards the door and tried to catch Dad's eye, but he looked away quickly, like a downtrodden workhouse person, and polished harder.

Once back in the safety of the hall, I stared at the living room door. Presumably some sort of inspector was coming. But why? Maybe our living room was contaminated with a superbug? Maybe we were taking part in reality TV? No, Mum and Dad would never agree after what happened last time. (Although, I supposed Mum might agree to swap husbands.) And it couldn't possibly be guests. Dad would never stand for it!

Anyway, even if they were desperately trying to stop an outbreak of some sort, we still had to eat, didn't we? I mean, it was all very well but where was my tea?

I was just preparing a reasonable but firm speech about the unfairness of living in a house where I was totally dependant on other people and how my life was more like being a pet than a twelve-year-old human being when Joanna appeared at the top of the stairs.

My sister Joanna is like every shallow, dumb fifteen-year-old school girl in a high school movie (or she tries to be). It doesn't seem very likely that I'm really genetically related to her. Underneath her schoolgirl exterior I think she's probably a sort of giant leech crossed with a human who was brought into creation as part of a laboratory experiment, but who managed to escape and Mum and Dad took pity on her because Mum had always wanted a daughter of her own.

Joanna leaned over the banister. "Hello."

Now I knew I'd entered a parallel universe.

"Hel. . . Sorry, I can't bring myself to do that. Why are you talking to me?"

"You've been in there!?" She pointed dramatically at the living room. "You've seen what it's like!?"

One of the weird things about Joanna is that she makes everything sound like questions. Like the rest of the family, she was obviously a bit hysterical. It was down to me to try and stay calm.

"I think," I said gently, "that Mum may have had some sort of a breakdown. It's nothing to worry about – they do sometimes, I saw it on telly. They get this thing where they can't stop cleaning and have to go on medication until they go back to their normal cleaning levels."

"If *only*!"

I thought she was going to launch into more hysteria, but instead she looked tragically down at the banister rail.

"Jordan, there's no easy way to put this. I'm afraid you'll have to move out and stay somewhere else for Christmas."

"What?" My tummy was rumbling and nervous breakdown or not, sooner or later someone was going to have to feed me. . . Hang about! *WHAT?*"

"I'm afraid there's been a tragedy in the family and there's nothing else for it."

"No there hasn't! They're all fine. Well, Mum's gone a bit funny but—"

"Not them. It's poor dear Aunt Maureen. She's been taken very ill and died."

I don't normally pay much attention to relatives unless they're the sort that send you money and even then it's normally just the handwriting.

"Who?"

"Well I don't really know. The point is Uncle Derrick who was married to poor dear Auntie Maureen is having to come and stay."

Uncle Derrick. Hmm, that did ring a bell. Uncle . . . OH! I stared at her. "But that's impossible. Dad hates Derrick! Dulcie hates Derrick! Don't you remember when Derrick and poor dear Auntie whatsit came for Christmas and Dad drank all of Dulcie's special Christmas whatever and ended up being really insulting with quite a lot of bad swear words and Mum had to pour a jug of wate. . ." I stopped and my eyes narrowed. "But getting back to the me-moving-out bit."

"Well." Joanna suddenly went all businesslike. "Due to poor Uncle Derrick's terrible bereavement, I felt I had to offer him my bedroom and so, obviously, I've had to move into your room. But it was, like, just the worst sort of mess? So I very kindly packed a bag for you. . ."

". . .So you see," explained Mum, who still looked like she'd been struck by lightning but was at least talking normally in an attempt to break up the argument, "you and Joanna will have to share while Derrick is here."

"But it's my room," I explained reasonably. "Joanna will just have to go and stay with friends. In fact she might find she enjoys it so much that she never comes ba—"

"Jordan!" Mum gritted her teeth.

"A tent!" I cried. "We'll put up a nice tent for her in the garden and decorate it with Christmas lights and—"

"JORDAN!"

"Jordan can go into kennels?" suggested Joanna.

"You can go and live in the reptile house. . ."

Mum doesn't often throw things when she's angry but the way she swept the vase off the mantelpiece crushed us into silence.

"Sorry, Mum," said Joanna in a sickly-sounding voice.

"We all appreciate how hard it is for you." She did one of those pauses that isn't quite long enough to let

14

anyone else get a word in. "But you know, there is a way round this. Jordan can share a room with Auntie Dulcie!"

She beamed like she'd just discovered electricity.

I thought about this. Dulcie is my favourite family member and it would be better than sharing with Joanna. Then again she was also really old and might have weird old-person type habits. And, I mean, no one likes to have to face this sort of thing, but there was always the risk that she might die in the night.

For some reason, Dulcie didn't seem too keen on the idea either. "I think the best thing to do would be to put me in a home for the duration," she said haughtily.

"If we had the money to put you in a home we'd have done it years ago," said Dad, which was unusually harsh even for him. "And if we could afford kennels I know the first person who'd be going there." He glared at Dulcie's Pekinese dog, Nemesis, who gave him a death stare back.

Mum sighed. "Look, all this squabbling isn't going to help. I was put on the spot and couldn't say no, OK? With any luck your Uncle Derrick will feel better in a few weeks and be able to go home."

"But –" I looked confused "– I don't get it. I mean . . . if poor Uncle Derrick has just lost poor dear Auntie Thing, then I don't see how him coming to stay in a house where everybody hates him is going to help."

Mum rolled her eyes. "Well I must admit I was a bit surprised when your cousin Janet asked, but she'd already booked a cruise so she couldn't have him. And it seemed that quite a few members of the family had already planned to go away. . ."

"CON-veniently!" said Dad loudly.

Mum ignored him. "Under any other circumstances I'd have made an excuse." She gave Dad a bit of a look. (Dad's pretty much used up every excuse in the book.) "But I wasn't about to leave Derrick on his own under such sad circumstances, especially at this time of year."

"Well!" said Dad crossly. "I'm. . ." Bravely he plonked down his spray polish, but then he caught Mum's eye. "Going to go and get some fish and chips!" he muttered pathetically.

Gotta hand it to him, when Dad rebels he really does it in style. While other men marched the streets armed with sticks ready to overthrow an evil dictator, there my dad would be, down the chip shop.

Three

He must have been gone about a quarter of an hour when there was a sound like a helicopter trying to land in the street.

I suppose it's something about living in a small village, but we have this gene which means nothing should ever happen (and especially not on our road) without us knowing about it. Me, Joanna and Mum all charged into the front room (which we're not meant to go in except on special occasions), with Dulcie tottering after us. We all peered out of the window. Outside in the darkness, a huge lorry was blocking out the moonlight. The back was down and some men were carrying a sofa up our garden path. Mum ran to open the front door and they almost barged her over.

"Excuse me," said the first one briskly as they shuffled off down the hall. He stopped outside the living room. "You'll be wanting this in here, will you?"

Gathering outside on the road was a growing collection of furniture. My mouth dropped open. Not only had Mum developed a serious cleaning disease because of Derrick, she'd ordered a whole truckload of new furniture for him as well. Dad moans if she even so much as buys a new cushion. When he saw this lot he was going to go mad.

Worse still, the headlights of Dad's builders van had just appeared at the top of our road. I looked round frantically for somewhere to hide.

Too late. Outside in the front garden, I heard the distinctive growl of Dad's voice.

"In here, love?" asked one of the sofa men again as they tried to angle the sofa into the living room.

"NO," I told him urgently. "You must take it back to the shop and get us a refund straight away."

I cringed as Dad's large bulky shape appeared in the doorway. It was hard to believe it but he seemed to be laughing. "Oi! It's next door, you pillocks."

The sofa men, looking a bit relieved, shuffled back out again and Dad came in grinning with his arms full of fish and chips. "Looks like our new neighbours have arrived then."

By nine that night, me and Dad were standing shivering in the dark on the neighbour's doorstep with a couple of toilet rolls.

Basically, Mum had decided to try and be neighbourly (which really means nosey), but she didn't have the courage to stick her beak in herself, so she sent us instead.

Dad had just started to look hopefully back at the front gate when the door opened. A boy who looked a couple of years older than me peered out. He had dyed black hair with a bad fringe and a long white face. I nodded at him in a friendly way, but he just peered even more.

"Is your mum or dad in?" Dad asked politely.

A skinny little man dressed all in black appeared. He had grey hair, a beard and round green-tinted glasses. He gave Dad a squinty little smile. "Can I help you?"

"Dominic Smith," Dad told him, "and this is my boy Jordan. We live next door."

Now the door was open a bit wider I had a bit of a nose inside but all I could see were a load of large wooden packing cases piled up in the hall.

"Ah!" said the man. He took Dad's hand in a limp handshake. "I'm Harold. And this is my son Xathian."

He said this like "Zaythian".

I pulled a polite face (after all you can't help what they call you), but Dad, who was obviously getting a bit impatient, shuffled and wiped his handshake hand on his trousers.

"Nice to meet you. Er. . ." He nodded embarrassedly at me. "My wife said to give you these and ask if you wanted a cup of tea bringing round."

I held out the toilet rolls. "Just in case," I explained

helpfully. "We didn't know if you might have been expecting shops – only there aren't any round here – at least there is one, but not at this time of night. Actually it quite often isn't open in the day either because the shop owner has lots of diseases, but don't worry, they're mostly made up. Anyway, Mum thought, you know, if you needed to go and you hadn't brought any. . ."

"Tea!" said Dad in a jolly voice. "Would anyone like a cup of tea?"

Harold dithered. "Have you any Earl Grey?" he enquired politely.

"No-o," said Dad also politely, but a bit too much if you know what I mean. "Normal."

"Just a sec." Harold held up a finger. "I think I know where to lay my hands on some." He came back a minute later with a handful of tea bags. Dad, who had started to glower, folded his arms and puffed impatiently. Harold shoved the tea bags at Dad.

"Have one yourself. You might develop a taste for it."

While all this was going on, Xathian leaned forward and whispered something to me. What he said was so weird it took a minute to sink in. Meanwhile Dad had decided enough was enough.

"Right." He shoved the tea bags back at Harold. "That's your lot."

Dad (who was saying quite a lot about his opinion of the new neighbours by not saying anything at all), was just about to stomp back up our own path when I tugged at his sleeve.

"That boy asked me if I'd ever drunk blood."

"That would be when you're not drinking your *Earl Grey*, would it?" He obviously wasn't listening properly.

Four

It wasn't until lunch break at school the next day that I got around to telling the others about our new neighbours. We were sitting on our favourite out-of-the-way bench eating fizzy colas.

"They're weird," I explained. "They wear all black and the dad creeps about like a skinny little gremlin. As for that vampire kid, Xathian, he looks like someone just dug him out of a grave."

"Is it just them?" asked Boy Dave. "Or is there a whole nest of them, d'you think?"

"Could be. There were loads of wooden boxes in the hall. Maybe that's how they transport themselves during daylight. Mind you," I added. "If they are a nest of vampires, they're very snobby ones."

"Yeah, the tea thing's really snobby," agreed Boy Dave. "Fancy giving you their own tea bags as if yours weren't good enough."

I nodded. "It was just as well Harold never gave us their own cups or Dad really would have lamped him."

"Perhaps they were special tea bags?" suggested

Ryan. "I mean, I suppose in lots of ways, being a vampire is like any other sort of allergy. Nowadays you can probably get all sorts of special biscuits and whatnot for it."

"Well let's just hope they stick to eating them then," I said. "It's all very well having what might turn out to be a huge nest of vampires next door – and obviously a lot more interesting than the old miseries who used to live there – but that kid Xathian is seriously creepy."

"You never know," said Boy Dave, "maybe they'll come in through the window and feast on your Uncle Derrick."

"Unless he turned into one himself and started feasting on us," I pointed out.

"What's he like anyway?" asked Boy Dave. "This Uncle Derrick? I mean, maybe you're worrying too much. He might turn out to be really jolly and a good laugh. For all you know," he added, "he could have really bad wind that everyone has to pretend they haven't heard." He chuckled. "I always think that's really funny."

"It would be good if he was like that," I admitted. "But he's not likely to be very jolly under the circumstances. And –" another wave of gloom washed over me "– I would still have to share a room with Joanna."

Not even the funniest body noises could

make up for that. It had been bad enough just sharing a room with her *things*. I'd been woken in the middle of the night by an overpowering smell of strawberries from her bath stuff, and had only just managed to shut it out and get back to sleep when the hideous racket of some boy band on her musical alarm clock had woken me up again. I'd been sniffing myself secretly all morning in case some of the strawberry smell was still on me.

"You know this new kid next door," said Boy Dave suddenly. "Does he have longish black hair and wear a leather jacket?"

"Well I've only seen him once, but definitely could be. Why? D'you know him?"

"No, but I have a feeling I might be about to."

I followed his gaze across the schoolyard to where two older kids were heading our way. It seemed like Xathian had made a friend. Louse (Roddy Binks) is a creepy fifteen-year-old who splutters things to us younger kids like, "Out of the way you little squirt" (obviously reads too many comics) and "Ignorant little maggot". He's skinny with spots and his head is shaved almost bald, which is why he's called "Louse". He normally walks hunched over with his long khaki coat flapping out behind him, but today he had his arms across his chest, wrapping it round him mysteriously.

Xathian's skinny, pale face peered down at me. "Hello, you're the kid who lives next door, aren't you?"

Close to, he looked less like the undead and more like his squinty dad.

"And you're also the kid who lives next door," I said cautiously.

"Interesting, yes." He pretended to think about it. "A sort of reversal of what I said."

Louse drooped his eyelids at us over the top of his collar and, for him, stayed weirdly quiet. Xathian held his hand out to Boy Dave.

"My name is Xathian." He said his name meaningfully, like he was about to add a title – Lord of Darkness or whatever. Boy Dave gave him a suspicious look. (Kids who shake hands are pretty weird at the best of times.) Cautiously he reached out his hand and quick as a flash Xathian twisted his hand palm up and bent over it like a fortune-teller.

"You have good veins," he said in a creepy voice.

Boy Dave snatched his hand away disgustedly. Xathian snickered and offered his own hand to Ryan.

"Who are you?"

"I'm Zarathustra," Ryan told him politely. "I have a rare skin complaint which means I must never touch the skin of another human being. If I do their flesh will burn like fire and slough off until the raw sinews beneath are exposed."

Xathian blinked but Louse, obviously forgetting he was meant to be dark and mysterious for a minute, sneered, "That little maggot is Ryan. And the other pipsqueak is David."

"Did you and your new slimy mate want anything in particular?" asked Boy Dave tiredly. "Or did you just get bored of playing on your own?"

Xathian raised his eyebrows and he and Louse gave each other meaningful looks.

"It must be terrible," said Xathian pityingly, "living the same mundane, normal little lives day after day."

He squidged revoltingly in next to me on the bench.

"Don't you ever imagine . . . Gordon. . .?"

"Jordan."

"Don't you ever imagine the . . . night? Embracing your limbs. . ."

Whatever weird and mysterious thing he was about to say was spoilt by Louse snatching the bag of fizzy colas off my lap and going, "What's this then? Ahh, my favourites," and cramming a load into his mouth.

He held the bag out to Xathian. "Have a sweet!"

Xathian gave him a dirty look. "I'm a sanguinarian, remember?" He looked snootily into the bag. "Fizzy colas don't . . . satisfy my . . ." He flicked his eyes creepily. ". . . *cravings*."

"Urrggh," said Boy Dave with a shiver as we made off fast. "Creep isn't the word."

"What's sang . . . whatever?" I asked.

"Blood drinker," explained Ryan casually.

Me and Boy Dave stared.

"For real?"

Ryan grinned. "Doubt it. I reckon underneath all that weirdness he's extremely normal and boring."

"But why would anyone pretend to be like that?" I asked, amazed.

"Maybe no one pays him any attention otherwise."

"I don't understand that at all. I'd love it if no one paid us any attention. We could get on with our lives so much better."

Boy Dave glanced back to where Xathian and Louse were sitting hunched over like two scabby bats on our bench. "Well he's managed to impress one person at least."

"Yeah," I said disgustedly. "But that's probably only because he admired his veins."

Five

Talking of vampirey, bat type stuff, that Saturday was Halloween. In our village we don't have street lights so we all carry torches, which is great for atmosphere.

On the subject of atmosphere, though, this year there was a bit of a snag. Following the horrificness of last year's Halloween (and obviously trying desperately to avoid *The Sequel*), the village hall committee, along with the Women's Institute and our school, had hatched a plan. Local kids were to be given a special "dressing up" party at the youth club to "keep us off the streets". Everyone had to have their name ticked off like the register at school. Meanwhile the village policeman, PC White, was going to be "patrolling throughout the night". They'd called it the "Hatton Down Zero Tolerance Campaign".

In case you're wondering what hideous carnage was so bad last year that this year they were locking us all up, here are some examples from the local paper. Unusually for our local paper the headline was quite dramatic:

TERROR RAMPAGE IN VILLAGE ON HALLOWEEN!

Picture 1: Issac from the newsagent's holding a banana with a grim expression on his face. Title: LOCAL SHOPKEEPER'S BANANA IN EXHAUST PIPE SHOCK! "The loud bang from my car almost shocked the life out of me," said local shopkeeper, Isaac Isford.

Picture 2: Mrs Bagnall from the Women's Institute holding out a dustpan and brush. Title: LOCAL WOMAN TERRORIZED BY BROKEN EGG. "I could easily have slipped on it!" Mrs Bagnall told *The Express*, "and had an accident."

Picture 3: Mrs White (PC White's mum) and her Pekinese dog, Confucius, looking bad-tempered with an orange balloon tied to its tail. Title: ANIMAL CRUELTY. "I don't know how anyone could do this to a poor defenseless creature," said Mrs White, the dog's owner.

Picture 4: The vicar standing beside a basket of sinister-looking squashes, turnips, pumpkins and courgettes with big evil-looking marker pen eyes. Title: CHURCH VANDALIZED ON HALLOWEEN. "Imagine the shock of my congregation," said local vicar, "when they came in to see the entire harvest display staring at them unpleasantly."

Me, Ryan and Boy Dave were particularly shocked at this last one.

Obviously this was all a big front so that the Witches' (cover name "Women's") Institute could get on with their special night undisturbed. On the other hand, the village hall, where the youth club is held, is an ancient, rickety old building with windows that rattle. You only have to bang against the wall and a bit of it falls off. Bunking out of one of the rooms behind the stage would be easy. In this respect having our names on *the list* could turn out quite useful.

By seven that night me, Boy Dave, Ryan, Claire and Daisy were making our way down the main street on our way to the village hall. Although Claire and Daisy live in the village, they don't go to our school. My dad said the place where they go is posh, but they're the most normal girls I know. Claire has long reddish-orangey hair and always wears jeans and bright T-shirts. Daisy has dark hair and is a bit more serious. She and Ryan have been really good friends since nursery.

It was Hilary on the door that night. I think she's about the only grown-up volunteer who actually enjoys being there – she's the sort who likes kids to come to her with their problems and gets really excited about having a "relationship of trust" with us all.

"Is there a band playing tonight then?" Boy Dave nodded through to the main hall. On the stage were a microphone and drum kit.

"Yes, they're called the . . . er. . ." Hilary peered at the banner slung across the front. "Vampire Death Squad. Very appropriate." She laughed and then did what she always does and explained the joke. "With it being this particular night I mean."

At least they couldn't be worse than the Christian youth band. You'd think they'd have known better than to have tambourines.

Claire and Daisy "volunteered" to do the tuck shop, chucking Steven Longacre and Isambard Cray out. They slid us over a few sneaky bars of chocolate and I looked round the rest of the hall. There were the usual werewolf and ghost masks. Connor Keefe, our class bully, with his usual "axe through the head", and Callum Mockford, his sidekick, as Frankenstein – oh no, tell a lie – Callum with no mask. Hmm, that was unusual: lots of older kids with their faces painted white and black eyes. By the looks of it, some had even dyed their hair black.

"Blimey," said Boy Dave. "What are all the depressed pandas doing here?"

"Isn't that your sister?" Ryan nodded towards a corner of the hall.

I groaned. "Oh no, it is as well."

Joanna never normally goes to youth club. Most of

the time she makes a big thing about it being "too childish".

She was with her mate Collette. They were wearing witches' hats and black miniskirts. They were with a load of other kids from their year. Not that you'd have recognized them. Kevin Mockford, Cal's older brother, had gone from looking like a normal pink pig to a white spotted pig with big patches around his eyes. He'd swapped his old puffa for a leather jacket. His mate Matty Haycock had the same make-up but looked like he'd dyed his hair black as well. Colette's bother Jamie had done it the other way round and painted his eyes and lips white and looked like he was about to try voodoo. The girls were mostly a bit more normal-looking except for Danielle Romney (who's always a bit pale anyway). She'd done purple eyes and hair and just looked like she'd been in a fight.

The lights in the hall dimmed to darkness until only a spotlight was left on stage. Seconds later Xathian and Louse ran on stage.

We goggled as Louse settled himself behind the drum kit and let out a loud raggedy drum roll. And to our total disbelief Joanna's corner let out a cheer.

"HELLO HATTON DOWN!" yelled Xathian.

Six

I'll say this for Xathian: with his straight black, greasy hair, goth make-up and long leather coat, he was really trying to look the part. He stretched out his arms. "Vampire Death Squad welcomes you!"

At the back of the room, Joanna and Collette screamed excitedly and me, Boy Dave and Ryan started to giggle.

"ARRAGHARRAGHARRAGH," yelled Xathian suddenly down his microphone. He thrashed his guitar wildy. "ARRAGHARRAGHARRAGHARRAGH ANTICHRIST ARRAGHARRAGH DE-E-EATH." There was a bit of a gap while Louse dropped his drumstick.

"ARRAGHHARRAGH," began Xathian again, after turning round and glaring at him. "NIGHTMARE ARRGGH VAMPIRE!"

"Blimey," yelled Boy Dave, "it's awful."

"It's the worst thing I've ever heard," I yelled back, wiping away tears of laughter.

While Joanna's lot seemed to be loving it and from our point of view it was hilarious, not everyone agreed. A small group started to form around Hilary in the entrance trying to leave. You had to hand it to the Hatton Down Zero Tolerance Campaign. Not only had they managed to trap us all inside the village hall, they'd found a way of torturing us while we were there.

I was just about to suggest that maybe we should chip off too (only out the back window) when Boy Dave nudged me. Joanna, Collette and some of the other girls had moved to the middle of the hall. With completely serious expressions they were writhing and waving their arms like they were pretending to be seaweed.

Me, Boy Dave and Ryan looked at each other. On the one hand it was the funniest thing we'd seen for ages. On the other hand, though, it was weird how Xathian had only been at our school a week and yet seemed to have got all these people around to his way of thinking.

As the first track squealed to an end, Joanna and the death pandas howled happily, but more and more of the rest of the audience were looking restless. I'm afraid to say that during the second track, which was exactly the same as the first one except that this one was called "Prowl the Night", a few bits of wet bog roll got thrown.

When it finally shrieked to a finish there was a bit of hostility.

"Oi!" yelled a big-looking kid in a werewolf mask."Get the pool table out."

"Yeah, go home," yelled the rest of his gang.

Joanna's lot shuffled nervously as Xathian put the microphone close to his mouth.

"*I'm coming to get you*," he said in a creepy voice.

"I'll be coming to get you if you don't **** off," yelled back the werewolf, whose mates had gathered around him.

"Er, this one's called 'Feast on Me'," said Xathian hurriedly.

"Woooo," went the death pandas.

"ARRARRGH ARRAGH BLOOD FEAST," began Xathian.

"GERRROFFF!" yelled the werewolves.

Lumps of bog roll and empty drinks cans flew through the spotlight.

"ARRAGHARGHullmph." A wodge caught Xathian in the mouth and the werewolves cheered loudly.

"DEATHARRAGHVEINSARRAGHARRAGH. . ." (Drink can.) "ARRGHHH OW!" Xathian howled for real.

With an unusual burst of disappointing sensibleness, Hilary bustled down and pulled out the plug.

Feeling extra cheerful after such a brilliant laugh, me, Boy Dave and Ryan were just about to and find something Halloweeny to do when the great star himself wandered over to the tuck shop. Underneath his make-up Xathian was looking unusually red and sweaty. He had a towel draped over his shoulders.

"Hi there." He gave Claire and Daisy a slimy smile. "Can I get a cup of water?"

He didn't seem to realize that his gig had been a total disaster. Claire pushed a squishy plastic cup of water across the counter. "Careful. It's a bit full."

"Oops," said Xathian as he squished the cup (to my mind deliberately) so water sploshed down his T-shirt. "Well you did warn me."

I don't really want to describe the next bit. Basically there was a bit of a conversation between Claire, Daisy and Xathian (but mainly between Claire and Xathian) where Xathian pretended to think he wasn't very good, but somehow managed to blame Louse for anything really bad.

"But hey." He gave Claire a smile so slimy it would have made Fungus The Bogeyman look dry. "I'll play with anyone just so long as I'm making music."

"That wasn't music," I told him. "That was just a really bad, loud noise."

He shrugged. "I kinda like the raw feeling – like sort of goth-screamo fusion. But I guess I have to be in the right zone." He turned back and leaned his elbow against the tuck shop. "I'm just as happy to knock out a blues or jazz riff," he told Claire coolly.

"What, like you were almost knocked out a minute ago?" suggested Boy Dave. "When they all started throwing things."

"There's always a few disbelievers," said Xathian mysteriously. His black eye paint was running freakily into the white like a tragic sort of clown. "We learn to transcend the haters."

It should have been funny. Except to me, right then, he really wasn't. I just couldn't believe how anyone as pathetic as him could think he was so great. It got worse.

"I'll give you my cell and you give me a call." I did a slimy impersonation. "Urggh I don't know how you could!"

We were hiding from PC White's "patrol" behind one of the big tombs in the graveyard.

"Shut up," said Claire crossly.

But it was hard to stop myself. "I kinda like it raw," I said in a stupid Xathian voice.

Boy Dave put his hand over my mouth.

"OK," said Ryan sternly. "What shall we do? We can't let Halloween just pass us by."

I managed to unpeel Boy Dave's hand. "So far as I'm concerned I'm all creeped out already!"

"You are?" said Daisy indignantly. "What about us?"

"I thought you liked him," I said sulkily.

Claire shot me a disgusted look. "Get lost! We thought it was funny, that's all."

"And we do have his mobile number," said Daisy nicely. "And it is Halloween."

While the possibilities of this sank in, Boy Dave looked at me strangely. "Happy now?"

Funnily enough, we actually did spend most of Halloween off the streets. We were round at Ryan's, busy arranging regular gardening and cooking tips and other un-gothy type stuff to be sent to Xathian's mobile. Along with a few calls and texts pretending to be from embarrassing clinics.

Seven

Straight after lunch on Sunday we headed excitedly for the Old Manor Hotel. It had taken quite a few overnight leavings-on to even get a layer of water in the swimming pool, but we reckoned that we might finally have filled enough for our ice rink.

It was nice in the woods. The sun was going down and the last of its rays lasered through the branches of the trees like thin spotlights. We passed through them as we scuffed the leaves. We were telling Claire and Daisy about Ryan's fireworks idea.

"It sounds great," said Claire. "But if you really want to make money you should sell soup."

"They won't be thinking of *soup*," said Ryan crossly. "They'll be too busy watching the amazing display."

"But everyone knows that's where you make the real money," said Daisy. "On the food. Even at the biggest events."

"If you get loads of tins of tomato soup and some French sticks," said Claire, "you could probably double your profit."

There was a bit of an embarrassed silence while me and Boy Dave (and maybe even Ryan) felt a bit stupid.

"We're not really used to soup," said Boy Dave doubtfully. "Aren't you meant to heat it up or something?"

"It's quite simple." Ryan waved his hand. "Claire and Daisy can put some soup in a big vat and if people want some they can have it cold with a bit of bread to dip. The most important thing is the display."

"We might," said Daisy sternly, "put soup in a big vat if we get a cut of the profit."

"Whatever," said Ryan in a superior way. "If it'll stop you going on about it."

"You can have a go of the fireworks too if you like," I offered generously.

They gave each other a particular sort of "girl look".

"These would be Ryan's extreme fireworks, would they?" asked Daisy, and Claire giggled. "If we decide to blow ourselves up between now and then," she said. "We'll let you know."

Ryan, who had started to look a bit offended, opened his mouth.

"Oh they're not dangerous," I said hurriedly. "On a scale of one to ten they're only a four. That's pretty good."

Daisy raised an eyebrow, but Claire said the same as me: "Well at least it's the right side of five."

By the time we'd scrambled over the wall to the pool, the courtyard and old stables were looming, eerie grey-blue in a dusky mist. From the pool came the faint sound of trickling water.

Boy Dave tapped the hose with his toe. "It's still working, then."

I lifted the edge of the tarpaulin. "It's too dark to see. Give me a stone."

Seconds later there was a faint plop. We let out a quiet cheer.

"Great," said Boy Dave. He went over and turned off the tap. "Finally!" There was a loud bang in the distance and we looked up to see a flash of green in the misty sky. "What a waste." He shook his head. "Letting fireworks off in the mist."

"It's a good night, though," I said. "We should go along the river, it'll be like it's made of smoke."

"We won't be able to see it by the time we get there," said Claire, shivering. "I reckon we should hang out in Boy Dave's garage instead."

I had to admit it was tempting. Boy Dave's garage is done up really nicely with beanbags and a little fridge full of fizzy orange. We sometimes buy chocolate to put in there but it never lasts long enough to get cold.

"Come on then." I turned and froze.

I'd been vaguely aware of an unusual shape on top of the wall – a squirrel maybe, or a small cat. But as I got nearer it shifted and stared down at me like an impaled head. Then it disappeared.

I thought I heard the faint sound of running but it quickly faded away.

"What's up?" Boy Dave's voice sounded behind me.

I stared at the empty space on the wall where the head had been.

"Someone was there," I said, without turning round. "Watching us."

A few seconds later, Boy Dave and Daisy jumped down from the wall.

"No one there, now," said Boy Dave.

"It was probably just a squirrel," said Daisy, "with its tail curled round."

"No." I shivered like someone had just walked over my grave. "It was a head."

"Probably just kids like us," said Claire. "Being nosey, that's all."

We spent the last hour before tea in Boy Dave's nice warm garage planning our fireworks display. Me, Boy Dave and Ryan agreed to make some flyers and Claire and Daisy agreed to sort out soup and a barbeque to heat it on. The main thing now was to decide where to have it. This was the tricky bit, because although we live in the countryside with loads of fields and so on, they're either guarded by the really vicious farmer or too public, like the village green.

In the end, we agreed to all think about it and meet up in a few days time to see what we'd come up with.

I went home that night with a creeping feeling of excitement.

Talking of creepy, I literally bumped into Xathian outside his front garden.

"Oi, watch it!"

"Sorry," I mumbled. "Didn't see you."

There was a creak as he opened the gate. "But I saw you. At the hotel."

Luckily it was misty and he couldn't see the look on my face.

"I dunno what you're going on about," I said casually.

"Yes you do." He sounded sly. "Me and Roddy were on our way home and we saw you and your little mates rushing off into the woods so we thought we'd come with. You know, join in the fun. Maybe help you get in touch with your 'were' sides."

"*What?*"

"Like werewolf?" said Xathian, as if I was stupid.

43

"We all have a 'were' side. You just need to know how to tune in to it."

"You need to get a life," I told him crossly as I opened my garden gate. "By the way, you do know you're totally weird, don't you?"

Xathian put on his silly, creepy voice. "More weird than you'll ever know."

I banged my front door loudly shut behind me. *Eeauch!* Even talking to the freak made me feel like I was crawling with maggots. And I could have kicked myself for telling him he was weird. He'd loved that. I hadn't meant it that way, though. I'd meant pathetic creep sort of weird. I mean, what was he doing, following us around, interfering in our business anyway?

It suddenly dawned on me that the house was totally dark. I tried the light. Not a power cut then; everyone must just be out. This was ridiculous! That was two nights now that I'd come home to find my tea not on the table. At this rate I'd be taken into care.

Mum had left a note on the table.

Taken Dulcie shopping – only chance I'll have. If not back make sandwich. Derrick arriving tonight! DO NOT MAKE A MESS!!!! Love Mum x

Oh no, it was really happening. I was going to have

to share a room with Joanna! And in the meantime I was somehow supposed to make myself a sandwich without making any mess. Still, there was one tiny little silver lining in this huge, grey cloud – at least I could make a sandwich the way I liked it for once.

Recipe in case you want to try it:
* Three slices of bread
* Peanut butter
(This does work – trust me.)
* Tomatoes
* Ham
* Pickle
* Crisps
* Coleslaw
* Cheese
* Lettuce
* Chilli sauce (drops)
Instructions: Arrange as sandwich.

I had just made my huge whopper slopper of a sandwich and sprawled out in an armchair with one leg over the armrest when Dad, Mum and Dulcie came back from Dulcie's shopping trip.

From their expressions, I got the feeling it hadn't gone very well.

"Right!" said Dad to Mum before Dulcie had even

managed to creak her way up the garden path. "I'm off down the pub."

Surprisingly, Mum seemed quite sympathetic. "All right, love," she said. "You get off, but you'll have to be back by seven for Derrick, remember?"

Dad looked at her as if he'd just caught his foot in a rabbit trap.

"And one pint only!" said Mum, who obviously thought he'd had quite enough sympathy for one day. Now I came to think about it, she was looking a bit frazzled herself.

Dulcie, who had finally managed to make it into the living room, lowered herself slowly on to the sofa. She must have seen her shopping trip as an "occasion" because she was wearing her best funeral coat and had her walking stick with the silver bird's head.

"So," I asked cheerfully, "what did you get?"

"I'll put the kettle on, shall I?" said Mum tightly.

"The problem is, Jordan dear –" Dulcie feebly tried to unbutton her coat "– wretched buttons, I don't know why they don't make things with hooks any more – that the shops are filled from floor to ceiling with cheap rubbish. As you know, I don't approve of plastic unless it's proper Bakelite, and nicely crafted wood is very hard to come by. Then, of course, there's all those awful lotions and potions that they try to palm one off with and there's far too much wrapping and boxes. . ."

"Did you . . ." I asked eventually, when she paused halfway through saying that one couldn't even get a proper pot of tea in this day and age. ". . . er, actually buy anything at all?"

Dulcie sighed. "I think I'm going to have to resort to the more traditional aspects of Christmas this year, Jordan dear."

"You mean just give people money and tokens and that?"

Mum, looking a bit grim, came in with a cup of tea and plonked it down beside her.

"Unless," said Dulcie loudly, "I can find a way of getting up to some proper shops in London, I shall just have to make my own presents. In the old days that's what we always used to do. There was none of this terrible commercializing of Christmas as there is now. My mother used to make a very nice non-cook chutney, and there's always pickled onions and cranberry sauce. I might even do some floral watercolours."

I nodded encouragingly. It would be great if Dulcie could get everyone round to her way of thinking. Instead of having to get thirty quid from somewhere, I could knock up a few paintings.

I was just about to say that I totally agreed that for over-fourteens it was the best thing you could give them, when the door opened slowly and Joanna, looking unusually moody and depressed (but also weirdly pleased with herself), slid through it.

Eight

Me and Mum stared at Joanna and Dulcie got her glasses out and held them up to her eyes without putting them on. The silence (unless you count me trying not to laugh) was finally broken by the sound of a car drawing up outside.

Mum, who had already gone pale at the sight that greeted her, went the colour of sour milk. "Derrick!" she whispered, and went to open the front door.

I should say at this point that Mum might have turned sickly yellow, but Joanna looked like death. Then again that was probably the idea. Her normally curly brownish hair was jet black and straight. It hung limply around her now chalk-white face like a wig made of oily string. All round her eyes and lips was black. She was wearing a ripped-up short black dress and shiny high-heeled ankle boots with torn black fishnet tights.

There was the sound of cases being plonked down in the hall. Dulcie had put away her glasses and was telling Joanna about the Gothic movement of the eighteenth century, but I was more interested by the stomach that had appeared at the edge of the living room door.

The rest of Derrick arrived slowly – like a sort of rising sun. When he had finally all entered, he was the nearest a real human could ever get to being a Mr Man. Derrick had short, stumpy legs and a bald, helmet-shaped head that looked as if it had been jammed into his body. His cheeks, which were droopy and mournful-looking, flopped on either side of his mouth, which was shaped like a flabby kiss. A pair of tiny little gold glasses perched on top of his nose like an insect.

Without looking at anyone and without waiting to be asked, he made his way straight to Dad's armchair and lowered himself down importantly.

Mum, who was still a sickly pale-yellow colour, followed him in. "Yes, do take a seat Derrick," she said in a faint voice. Then she carried on staring at Joanna.

Joanna, who was obviously torn between loving the attention and being a bit nervous of Mum, went, "Look, just because I decide to be different. . ."

"OK, stop there." Mum took a deep breath. "Is there . . ." she said this next bit slowly "by any chance . . . the faintest hope . . . that you could wash that black out of your hair before your father gets home?"

Joanna looked surprised. "No of course not. It's permanent?"

I shook my head sorrowfully. "You'll never get her back now. She's totally transmogrified."

Derrick, who had been sitting stiffly at the edge of Dad's armchair, said in a dull, Scottish accent, "It will send poison into her head through the skin." He blinked slowly behind his insecty little glasses. "We absorb what we put on to our skin into our bodies."

Joanna went a bit pink. "It's not poison! It's hair dye."

"OK." Mum looked like someone who's about to make a parachute jump. "Here's what's going to happen. *You* are going to go upstairs and change into normal clothes. And you will not come down until *I* have had a chance to break the news to your father."

Joanna glared at her. "You can't tell me what to wear!" She looked down proudly at herself. "Our clothes are an expression of our inner selves? If you'd ever read the Geneva Convention you'd know that individuality is a basic human right."

Mum looked grimmer than she had done in a long time. "*Fine!* Sit down here and wait for him to discover you himself then. And after that you can both go into the garden and discuss the Geneva Convention."

I would like to say that me, Mum and Dulcie

waited in silence for Dad to come home, but that wasn't really the case. After Joanna went upstairs, Derrick started talking. He didn't actually *stop* talking for . . . well . . . he didn't.

Ever stop.

Nine

The next morning I met Boy Dave at Hangman's Lane for school.

"Whew." He gave me an up and down look as I staggered towards him. "You look rough."

I collapsed pitifully against a tree trunk. "I didn't get a wink of sleep last night. Joanna snores really loudly and just when I'd got used to that, she started laughing and talking in her sleep."

"Did she say anything interesting?"

"Don't be silly." I heaved myself back up and dragged along beside him to the village green. "It was exactly the same as during the day, but with the whole night ahead and no escape. Most of it was mumbling. I'd just dozed off when she said at the top of her voice, 'My lovely silver balloon' and let out a great cheer and started clapping."

"Did you ask what her dream was about?"

"NO! It was bad enough the first time round. Sorry, I'm going to need another rest."

We sat on the bench by the pond and watched the ducks for a bit.

"And if that wasn't bad enough," I said gloomily, "Derrick arrived yesterday and he's terrible."

Trying to explain the true terribleness of Derrick doesn't really work. I could have told Boy Dave that he was boring and dull and that after a bit his voice made you feel like a swarm of enormous gnats had been buzzing round your head for a week – but that wouldn't even come close. I've quite often thought that boredom is a sort of torture. Most of the time you can escape it by daydreaming, but there was something about Derrick's voice that meant you couldn't even do that.

I don't actually expect you to read all this next bit, by the way, but this is an example of Derrick (one long, drawn-out drone starting off with something that might have been to do with Joanna):

"I always think a young lady that is nicely turned out speaks well of her upbringing, these days so many young women look like something the cat brought in, but then of course they know no better, their heads are filled with nonsense about going out to work and doing a man's job when their place is in the home cooking and doing the chores to provide a comfortable place to which their menfolk can return home, I mean I have nothing against a touch of glamour for a night out. . ."

And getting on to (what was obviously his favourite subject) food:

". . .the meal we had in a very pleasant little restaurant right on the coast was perfectly decent for a place that size, I mean game is one of those dishes that is hard to do well and proper game potatoes are especially hard to come by, the oil they fry them in is often dirty. . ."

Leading to his other favourite subject of hygiene:

". . .I always think hygiene is so important and standards have slipped so since the days when a pot or a pan had to be properly scrubbed, nowadays they seem to be very unaware of the importance of hygiene in most walks of life but especially in food outlets. . ."

Now imagine that you are sitting in a room with him and that this is only one minute's worth of *HOURS and HOURS* of it. And I haven't even started on him talking about all the diseases that he comes across in his GP's surgery.

"Maybe it's the grief that's making him boring," suggested Boy Dave as we started off for school again. "It can affect people in many different ways, you know."

"Well that's the other thing – he doesn't seem to be in the least bit upset or grieving at all. It's like poor Auntie Thing never died at all."

"Hmm." Boy Dave looked wise. "He might need help opening up so he can talk about his loss."

I gave him a look. As far as I was concerned, if Boy Dave was going to go all sensitive and social-worky it ought to be about my terrible situation, not Derrick's.

"You are kidding! No one can get a word in edgeways – not even Joanna. We spent the whole time after her argument with Dad fighting about who should be allowed to hide in my room."

"Wow, your dad argued with Joanna? That makes a change."

"I know, he's normally dead scared of her and Mum. It's quite funny actually, Joanna's dyed her hair black and gone all goth like the rest of her class. I think it's something to do with that new kid Xathian." I had a sudden, creepy flashback. "Talking of which, I think we might have a problem."

When I'd finished telling Boy Dave about Xathian being "the head" at the Old Manor, he looked as surprised as I'd been.

"He can't tell anyone anything, though," he said eventually. "Because he doesn't know anything. And all this following us about is probably because he's new and doesn't know many people. Once he's got more mates he'll forget all about it."

I raised an eyebrow. "He's got quite a following already. And look what he's done to them."

"Yeah, true, but. . ." Boy Dave shrugged. "Anyway forget him." He nudged me. "Come on, cheer up."

We'd stopped in front of the school gates and he looked suddenly embarrassed. "Er . . . I don't want to be rude but I couldn't help noticing that you smell a bit funny. I wouldn't mention it. . ." He nodded towards the school. "Only I thought it would be better coming from me – you know."

I hung my head. "It's strawberries, isn't it?"

"Um . . . might be. Look, I'll tell you what, we're too late for first lessons now anyway. Why don't we take the morning off and go back to mine? My mum's gone into town so I can find you something to eat and we can decide a bit more about what we're going to do for the fireworks."

Ten

By the time we went back to school I was feeling a whole lot better. Me and Boy Dave had made banana milkshakes and eaten a mound of toast – with the butter on before it goes in the toaster so it really melts in.

"Poo," said Ryan when we caught up with him after lunch. "You smell like the inside of a taxi."

"Don't sniff me." I shoved him away. "It's rude."

"Joanna's stuff makes him smell of strawberries in the night," whispered Boy Dave tactfully. "So he's borrowed a little drop of my dad's aftershave." He did the "little drop" with his finger and thumb. If only! The truth was I'd been so desperate to stop smelling girly I'd dolloped it everywhere. It was like walking round in a vapour of *eau de dad*.

We'd been heading for the bench outside the school theatre. Most people forget it's there. It's down the side in a sunless alley and we don't normally use it, but Xathian, Joanna and the death pandas were on our usual bench. They were all hunched over with their coats wrapped around them like bat wings. It was probably only a matter of time before they started hanging from ceilings.

I realized recently that days are like little hills of good moments and bad moments. You kind of expect that if you've just had a bad moment and gone downhill, things will pick up again. Except today, things went even further downhill.

When we reached the alley, it was blocked off with plastic barriers. On a big notice was written **Rise Building Contractors**. It might as well have said "spies".

I groaned. We'd known our dads had got the contract to build the new school gym, but we'd kind of hoped they wouldn't be starting until the holidays. As if having to walk round smelling like them wasn't bad enough, the smothering ether of *eau de dad* was just about to materialize into the real thing.

We looked cautiously over the barriers. Their equipment was all lined up down the side of the wall but, so far, no sign of any people.

"They were probably just unloading today," said Boy Dave, dipping under the tape. "They must be finished now. Come on, we'll eat our sandwiches quickly and then hang out in the canteen or something."

"Your dads have got some very interesting things," said Ryan. He was crouched down beside what looked like a yellow box on wheels and was busy making notes in his notebook. "I don't suppose there's any chance they'd lend me some of this stuff?"

"You're joking," said Boy Dave through a mouthful of roll. "They won't even lend us a screwdriver if we want to change batteries. I have to use a knife."

"I use Joanna's nail file," I told him. "You can have it if you like. I can nick her new one."

"GERROUT!"

A sudden shout roared up the alley and two hideously familiar big shapes stomped towards us. Seconds later, my dad and Big Dave were standing over us with their arms folded.

"Son," Dad, having finally recognized me, nodded gruffly. "What are you doing here?"

"This is where I go to school?"

"Wrong!" He looked smug. "*This* is our building site."

"So you're starting work before the holidays then?" asked Boy Dave, trying to sound casual.

"Looks that way," said Big Dave. "We'll be able to keep an eye on you for the rest of term. Won't that be nice?"

They both laughed like he'd cracked some hilarious joke.

"Was there anything else?" asked Dad when he'd calmed down. "Before you clear off out of it?"

"No," we muttered.

We'd just stood up when Big Dave sniffed noisily. "Hang about! Have you been nicking my aftershave?"

Boy Dave went red. "Er . . . maybe. Like, just a little drop."

Surprisingly, instead of launching into the usual "You don't go messing with my stuff" routine, Big Dave and my dad raised their eyebrows at each other.

"Trying to impress anyone in particular, are we?" asked Big Dave.

"Maybe," muttered Boy Dave, going even redder.

Dad winked at him. "Good on you, mate!"

By now we were all for getting out of there as fast as we could, but just as we reached the end of the alley my dad yelled, "And don't forget; straight home after school tonight."

"*What?*"

I swung round but he and Big Dave had already disappeared through the side door.

I did try not going home but almost as soon as we were out of the school gates, Mum rang "just checking" I was on my way home.

"Derrick?" she said crossly. "Meal? Honestly, Jordan, I told you about three times."

I was still racking my brains when she said (still irritably), "Derrick is taking us all out for a meal tonight as a thank-you for having him. I need you home to get ready straight away."

"But it'll only take me ten minutes to get ready."

"That's what I'm afraid of! This is a very swish restaurant we're going to and I don't want you showing us up!"

Eleven

It was about seven that evening when me and Dad met on the landing.

"The pain," he said heavily.

"Yes," I groaned. "It's like . . . ahhhh . . . knives. And I feel really sick."

"Oh dear. We'll just have to go for the meal without you."

"Really? I mean, ooaah."

Dad glared at me. "No, *not* really. You will come to this meal. And you will not put a foot out of line." He shot a disgusted look downstairs. "If you show me up in front of that stuck up . . . dollop I'll have your guts for garters, do I make myself clear?"

I knew what he meant. Over breakfast that morning Derrick had made quite a few comments about cowboy builders ripping people off, tramping "muck" around and ruining the garden. It had been like he was talking about a type of animal instead of actual human beings like my dad.

Still it had made a change from the "young ladies should behave like young ladies and not go moping round like death warmed up because their fathers will never get them 'married off'".

To Joanna, other people's voices are an unnecessary noise that get in the way of her own voice and I don't think she realized. Mum was fuming, though.

Derrick had then drearily said, "I was meaning to tell you, I heard *scratching* behind the walls last night."

"Don't worry," I told him. "That was just Joanna scrabbling to get out of her coffin."

"You scratching your nits, more like," said Joanna.

Derrick looked especially mournful. "You must have rats in your wainscot," he announced.

This was a new one. There had already been the moaning about the dust in the bedroom that made his chest bad, and Nemesis having fleas and carrying diseases into the house. He'd suggested to Mum that she buy a feather duster, and suggested to Dulcie that "the hound" be kept in a kennel outside. After the rats comment, he'd suggested that Mum put down rat poison and give the "whole place a good spring clean" and stop leaving household waste lying about. Which was especially bad when you think back to all cleaning she'd done before he even arrived.

I looked at Dad and sighed. "OK. I'll do my best at the restaurant, but I don't know why you don't just send him home."

"If he hadn't lost his wife, he wouldn't be here

in the first place, would he?" said Dad. "Think about it. Maybe we're better than that." Then he spoilt it a bit by saying, "Well, your mother is, anyway."

We made our way downstairs in gloomy silence.

A few moments later we made our way back upstairs again in an even gloomier one.

"The things I put out for you at the end of your beds!" yelled Mum from the hall.

As if wearing a suit that I'd most likely last worn to a wedding when I was about five wasn't uncomfortable enough, I had to go in the taxi with Derrick and Joanna. I'd never heard anything like it. It was like being trapped between two giant insects that had decided to drone to the death.

"And I mean we have so many sides to ourselves." (This was Joanna.) "Xathian – he's this amazing boy at our school – he says that I have a naturally dark soul and. . ."

"Of course the French serve cheese after the sweet," Derrick continued his own drone, "but I always think. . ."

"Xathian's 'were' side is really wild. He's a sleek, grey prowling wolf. . ."

"SHUUUT UUUP!" That was me. "Sorry, I think the driver might have taken a wrong turn." Either that or he was looking for somewhere to chuck us out because two of his passengers were insane.

Derrick peered through the front window. "No, this is it. They do rather a nice Roquefort, and I thought rather than. . ."

Nervously I eyed the grand-looking entrance of the Old Manor Hotel. I mean, it's not like they could possibly know about the ice rink or anything, but. . . I glanced nervously over at the old stables on the other side of the car park. Even though the hose was switched off it was like I could still hear the ghostly telltale sound of trickling.

"They do a set menu," Derrick started off boringly. In his suit and bow tie he looked more like a Mr Man than ever. "Consisting of starter, main course and sweet. Or one can have cheese and biscuits if one prefers. They do a Roquefort, which I think will be quite adequate with the port. . ."

I squished my fingers in the lobes of my ears and rubbed them like you do to get water out. By now it was like the giant insect was actually inside my head.

If it hadn't been for Derrick I would have quite liked the restaurant. There was a big roaring fire in the fireplace and tall grand windows, with heavy purple curtains. Every table had a thing with candles in it and the walls had large portraits of all the lords and ladies who'd lived there.

"Or melon," continued Derrick, "with Parma ham. . ."

Dulcie, who hadn't even had to listen to him on the journey here, fished a newspaper out of her bag and started doing her crossword.

"Dulcie, darling. . ." Mum gave her a warning look.

"One has to do something, Angela dear," said Dulcie irritably.

Not having a crossword, I gazed down the list of food and tried to concentrate on that instead. In films and such like there is normally a joke about not understanding the menu, but this one was in English. My problem was that I didn't understand the food. So far as I could gather, all the puddings and main courses were mixed together – meat with prunes, onion jam, cheese custard, prawn mousse. . . They were like the sort of stuff you concoct as a practical joke.

I looked up at Dad. His chin was pulled back and his eyebrows were raised. He looked like he does when he has to eat salad – only worse. I could guess how he was feeling.

Dad only likes about five things anyway, which are:

* Cooked breakfast
* Steak and chips
* Fish and chips
* Roast dinner
* Bangers and Mash

(And six if you count ham sandwiches).

I mean he likes fruit as well, but that's normally on its own or in puddings. Him not moaning must have meant he was really determined not to give Derrick an excuse to be snobby.

As the waiter took our order I peeked at the other tables. It was hard to tell what the people were actually eating, but they seemed to be enjoying it. So far as I could tell no one was spitting it out or running off to be sick. I started to feel a bit more cheerful. I'd been out in the cold all day and was really hungry. I mean, even if what I'd chosen turned out not to be very nice, it couldn't be that bad.

The food came.

Twelve

"Er. . ." I stared at the plate in front of me. It was a pile of tiny toasts beside a spoonful of what looked like dog poo with sprinklings of mouse poo on top.

"You spread it on with the little knife, darling," said Mum helpfully.

I looked round the rest of the table. Dulcie had a bowl of small black sluggy things sprinkled with leaves. Derrick was happily crunching on little fish with dead, staring eyes and Dad was scowling down at a large seashell full of sloppy bright-green liquid. Mum had gunky pink goo with prawn tails sticking out of it and Joanna had the same as me. She was waving her hands over it as if she was trying to magic it away.

"I don't think this is what I actually ordered?"

"Yes, sweetheart," said Mum. "Pate and truffles."

"Oh right," said Joanna lamely. "But like I thought. . ."

Like me she'd obviously just hooked on to the truffles bit. Seeing as how all the sweets and main courses were mixed up together we'd been hoping for chocolate. Still, maybe we were being a bit hasty. Perhaps this was chocolate which had just been melted down and mixed into a sort of thick and unpleasant textured heap. I bent down and risked a little sniff.

"URGGGH." I tried to blow the terrible smell back down my nose again. "Oh man, that is. . ." I caught Dad's eye. "So unusual," I spluttered.

Derrick looked pleased. "They have special pigs, you know, who search out the truffles from the undergrowth with their highly sensitive snouts. . ."

When the waiter cleared the plates, Mum said, "Very nice, thank you," and looked approvingly at mine and Joanna's empty dishes.

But I was starting to get seriously nervous about the main course. If that revolting gunk was their idea of chocolate, I hated to imagine the pancakes. Not only that, but I only had Mum's word for it that this was what crepes actually were.

In the event, by the time my "crepes" arrived, I didn't care what they were like – just so long as they shut Derrick up.

I looked down at the plate the waiter had just put in front of me. Tomato sauce, hmm; personally I think of chocolate sauce when I think of pancakes, but at least it was something I recognized. I smoothed a cautious gap in it with my fork.

Oh no.

"Do you think," I asked as politely as I could, "it's possible that my . . . things . . . might be mouldy?"

Dad was flipping irritably at a bit of puffy pasty on top of a tall, thin tower of meat. He glared at me.

"But they're *green*," I hissed.

Mum leaned over. "The green bits are herbs. I'm sure it's delicious," she said sternly.

I stared at her. This was ridiculous. First I was meant to eat gunk that had been gathered by pigs and now I was supposed to tuck into green pancakes. Well, so far as I was concerned, Derrick could be as snobby as he liked. I wasn't going to eat them and that was that. In fact, I was feeling really angry now – I wasn't going to put up with it a moment longer.

With Derrick and Dad fighting over who could scoff the most down before the other one could have it, I hadn't eaten properly for days and I was starving. Let them all force the horrible food down if they wanted to – but I'd had just about enough.

"Uncle Derrick," I said firmly. "It's very kind of you to take us all out and treat us to this lovely meal." Derrick stopped talking and peered mournfully at me through his glasses. "But I think I'll just have some cheese on toast when I get—"

"Hurrumph," Dad coughed loudly.

"HOME," I said even more loudly. "So if you could all be as quick as you ca—"

"HURRUMPH," coughed Dad, even more loudly.

"Only I'm very hungry and haven't eaten properly for days because. . . Urghmmph."

I couldn't believe it. Dad was trying to feed me.

"*TRY* it."

"Urghh, ummph. . ." I choked as I tried to gag the repulsive pancake up again.

"It looks so nice." Dad's eyes were rolling. Any minute now he was going to start foaming at the mouth. "*I'm* going to try it!"

Mum looked round the restaurant. "Well I must say," she said approvingly. "This is a rare treat for us all, Derrick."

"Not so rare!" said Dad through a big wodge of pancake. "We do eat at posh restaurants, you know."

He gave a gagging sort of swallow. "Mmm." He rubbed his tummy weirdly. "Great. Now go on. Tuck in."

Well at least I knew they weren't poisoned.

With lots of gulps of water and in between waves of hot and cold nausea I managed to get a bit down. I looked hopefully down at my dish. They were obviously magic pancakes that remade themselves as soon as you took a piece. I wiped my clammy forehead with the back of my hand. The way I saw it there wasn't much choice. I'd practically made myself sick and I hadn't so much as made a dent in them. And I was pretty sure the last thing Dad wanted was for me to throw up everywhere.

The pancake drooped tragically on the end of my fork like a speared fish as I shot a quick look round. Right, here goes. Quickly I flipped it into my other hand beneath the table and crammed it into my pocket.

The truffle heap must have started to seep through the napkin because the inside of my pocket was really soggy, but by folding the pancake up I just about squeezed it into the other one. With any luck, once my jacket was on no one would notice.

I sat back in my chair and poked the remains of the other pancake around my plate, but the slimy feeling on my leg was getting worse and worse.

I risked a quick look under the table. Oh wow. A hideous brown stain was seeping down my trousers. This was terrible. The repulsive food had started leaking.

I looked round for something to dab it with. Ahh, the edge of the tablecloth!

OK, that just smeared it about. Napkin! There used to be a napkin. . . But that was now wrapping up the truffle goo. Right – absolutely nothing to wipe the slime with. But I couldn't just leave it oozing out like that, it looked really bad.

I had to somehow get the gunk out of my pockets. And quick.

Thirteen

My jacket was over the back of my chair. With any luck, if I hunched over a bit. . .

"I'm just, er . . . off to the toilet."

Trying not to draw attention to myself I slid out of my chair. Then, hunched over with my hands in my pockets to contain the hideous squidges, I made my way, Quasimodo style, between the hundreds of tables.

But standing up had made it worse. By the time I reached the toilets, the goo was trickling into my socks.

Luckily it was the sort of toilet where the sink and loo are in the same room. I locked the door and leaned against it, relieved. Phew, now all I had to do was empty it all out and clean up a bit.

With a heaving stomach, I emptied the gunk and disintegrated pancakes into the bowl and flushed the chain. Yuck, the smell was still on me, but at least I could try and wash the worst of it off. Yanking off my trousers, I started scrubbing at the stain with a paper towel.

I was just rinsing out my pockets when a sudden gurgling noise made me turn round.

I froze. A hideous brown tide had begun seeping over the edge of the toilet bowl.

Frantically, I rushed over and flushed the chain again.

With eerie quietness, the brown tide went from seeping to pouring over the edge like a waterfall. Paralyzed with horror, I watched as it spread over my feet across the floor. OK, right! I had to stay calm. All I had to do was rush out and say we must leave at once – there were . . . cockroaches. And rats. And no one must eat another mouthful in case of disease. There was no time to wait for the taxi. We'd walk back through the woods. . .

I jumped as the door slammed shut in the ladies' next door. Oh no. What if it was Mum? What if she saw all the water coming from underneath my door when she came out?

Yanking the hand towel from the rail I threw myself down and slopped madly.

It was obviously a special sort of towel that didn't actually soak things up.

Maybe no one would know it was me? If I could only stop any of my family going to the toilet for the rest of the meal they might not. . . I put my head in my hands and groaned. There was no way. But what to do? Everything I tried just made it worse.

I slopped back to the sink and fished the mobile out of my clammy jacket pocket. If ever a situation required a touch of twisted brilliance, this was it.

Ryan's voice sounded very far away. I knew what it would be like now – to be all alone and injured on top of a mountain with only a mobile for contact with the outside world.

"I've got a problem," I whispered hoarsely, "and I seriously need your genius."

"You'll have to try and poke the food down," Ryan was saying as I poked feebly at it with the toilet brush. "The reason it's blocked is that you have tried to get too much stuff to pass round the. . ."

There was a loud bang on the door.

"Oh no," I hissed. "Someone's trying to get in!"

"OK, whatever you do, don't panic. Just say in a normal voice – 'I shan't be a moment!'"

"Shan't be a moment," I called in a strangled, unnatural-sounding voice.

"Jordan! Is that you?"

"This is dire. It's Joanna!"

"Tell her to go away."

"Go away."

"They're waiting for you to come back so they can order sweet. Mum asked me to find out where you were?"

"Well now you know."

"Jordan. Why is there, like, sewage coming from under the door?"

I stared despairingly to where the tsunami of brown water was slopping out into the corridor. If only everything would stop leaking.

"I'm going to tell Mum you've done something weird in the toilet."

"NO!" Quickly I turned the lock. Me and Joanna stared at one another and then Joanna stared at the floor, her eyes growing wider and wider.

"Oh . . . my . . . God. It's, like, really flooded? Is that. . .?"

"Nooo. It's just . . . the food," I finished lamely

"But, like, you haven't got any trousers on?"

"Because it got all down them," I hissed wildly. "Look, will you please just go away and let me handle it."

"You put your meal down the toilet?"

My shoulders sagged.

"Yes. And quite a lot of toilet paper. And maybe, accidentally, quite a big napkin. Look, I really don't have time for this."

"Hello-o," Ryan called at the other end of the line. "What's going on?"

"Sorry." I moved the phone back to my ear. "I'm having to explain a load of really obvious stuff to Joanna."

By now Joanna was really struggling with, on the

one hand, the huge temptation of dobbing me in, and on the other the excitingness of wanting to hang round and enjoy me being in a really bad situation.

"Who's that?" she asked interestedly.

"Ryan," I told her. "He was helping me."

"Listen," said Ryan at the other end of the phone. "I think I have the solution. From what you've said the toilet is too far gone to be unblocked. You'll just have to pretend it wasn't you."

I clutched at the phone. "And that's your brilliant solution?"

"Sorry," came the distant voice. "It's all I've got."

Joanna shook her head. "If anyone finds out about this, you are so dead."

Fourteen

"I've found him," said Joanna in an unnatural sing-song voice, which was especially unnatural seeing as she would never normally be so pleased about "finding me".

I gave a sickly smile and draped my crumpled jacket back over the chair.

"Good," said Mum, looking at us a bit oddly.

"We've already chosen," said Dad grumpily over the noise of Derrick. "You'd better hurry up or we'll be here all night."

I gazed down the sweet menu and tried to relax. Actually this didn't look too bad. There was even some normal stuff like apple pie and ice cream. And let's face it, after the deal I'd just struck with Joanna to keep her quiet I was going to need every little scrap of enjoyment I could get.

We ordered. Derrick droned. Dulcie got out her newspaper and started doing the crossword again. Mum gave up trying to be polite and leaned across and helped. At least my pockets were just a bit damp now. And it was quite nice here with the fire and candlelight. Well, it would have been if it wasn't for . . . wasn't for . . . that was strange!

Derrick had stopped droning.

In fact, Derrick had pushed back his chair and was standing up.

"But Uncle Derrick," I heard Joanna say, "why not wait until after. . ."

Too late. His podgy figure was already rolling purposefully across the restaurant. And from the look Joanna was giving me, there was no doubt where he was heading.

The waiter came and brought cutlery for dessert. I tried to concentrate on the way the candlelight was reflecting from my little fork – white flickers, dancing and twinkling . . . nothing to do with me, I'd say. No one could prove a thing and for once in her life Joanna would back me up.

Our desserts arrived. Mine actually looked like apple pie and cream. I tried a cautious mouthful. Great! It even tasted like it.

Mum said, "Derrick won't want us all waiting until he gets back; I think we'd better tuck in."

Me and Dad didn't need telling twice. As I shovelled down mouthfuls of yummy apple pie I felt almost jolly. The toilets must be all right again or else Derrick wouldn't have been in them for so long. I mean, there was no way someone as particular as Derrick would. . .

Derrick returned. There were two small red spots on his normally pale cheeks.

"I have just had to have very strong words with the manager!" he announced. "The bathroom is . . . is –" for the first time ever he was practically lost for words "– awash with . . . with . . . excrement! I have explained to the manager that his establishment is a disease-ridden, germ-festering. . ." Unable to think of anything terrible enough to call it, Derrick's eyes bulged scarily. "I have refused to pay for our meal. We are leaving at once!"

Quickly I crammed in the last of my apple pie and tried to avoid Joanna's eye.

"Derrick!" Mum looked shocked. "Whatever is the. . .?"

A managery-looking person appeared at our table. He had a waiter with him.

"It's no good," Derrick told him pompously. "We are leaving. And I shall be writing to the Department of Health!"

The waiter looked at me and whispered something to the manager.

"If I might have a word," said the manager in a low voice to Derrick.

With all the stress of what was going on, I hadn't paid much attention to the burning smell. But

80

suddenly there was a loud squawk and Dulcie went, "Oh dear! The candle! Oh dear, how foolish of me!" She was flapping her newspaper wildly.

Me and Boy Dave have had a quite few accidental fires in our time. Normally you just throw water on them. At the same time as Dulcie flung the, now-burning-merrily, newspaper on to the table I quick-thinkingly grabbed Derrick's glass and hurled the contents at it.

It was like setting fire to an oil well. As the smallish blaze became a ceiling-high column of whooshing flames, a panicked gasp went round the restaurant. There was the sound of chairs screeching and the manager staggered back clutching the top of his head.

"This way out, please," shouted the waiters. "This way out."

As for us, we stood like a group of shipwrecked sailors who had arrived on a hostile island and managed to light a table-shaped bonfire.

Seconds later there was a loud hiss and a waiter stood back, panting heroically. He was pointing a fire extinguisher at us like a machine gun.

The manager personally escorted us from the hotel, but it was difficult to take him seriously because he didn't have any eyebrows and his hair was all patchy.

Fifteen

The next evening after school there was a meeting about the fireworks in Ryan's mum's barn. Apparently Ryan's mum wasn't "doing" Christmas this year. Instead she was going to have a pagan festival. We were surrounded by pagan festival mushroom sculptures that she'd made specially. There was an upside-down dustbin with the lid on top, and an umbrella stuck into a traffic cone, but it was hard to make out what the rest of them were because they were all painted red with white spots. Clucking in between them were the pagan feast hens and outside in the yard was the pagan feast pig (whose fate I didn't really want to think about).

We were meant to be talking about our fireworks display but I was all for exploding myself. "It's really unfair," I told the others (for what might not have been the first time). "I mean, anyone would think I deliberately threw Derrick's drink on the fire to make it worse."

"If you throw alcohol on a fire," explained Ryan

patiently, "the effect is different from when you throw water on one."

"You don't say!" Even with my limited scientific talents I'd worked that one out. "Anyway, it's not just that. They don't seem to realize that you can't just give people something that was dug up by French pigs and expect them to eat it. I was trying to be polite. How was I supposed to know the toilet would go like that?"

Claire, who was sitting on top of one of Ryan's mum's mushrooms like a garden gnome, said gently, "The pigs only sniff to find the truffles, you know. They don't actually dig them up themselves."

"That's not the point! The point is that pigs choose food that they like. I mean, what if a cat goes and catches a mouse? What if a rabbit goes and finds a lump of grass? I'm meant to umph that down, am I? It's ridiculous. Anyway they do dig them up. Derrick said they have special spade type snouts."

"Well, whatever." Boy Dave sounded bored. "It's over with now."

"But it's not. I have weeks and weeks of it to go. And you should hear him droning on about the whole toilet, hygiene thing – and about me not appreciating good 'cuisine'. It's endless. Dad looks like he can't decide whose head to rip off first – mine or Derrick's. But I expect it would be mine because *I* haven't had a *bereavement*."

"Still, it sounds like Joanna wasn't too bad for once," said Boy Dave encouragingly.

"Not then," I groaned. "But she is sooo making up for it now. And the only reason she didn't tell on me when it happened was because A: she didn't want to leave the restaurant and B: I had to promise to say I wanted to sleep on the couch every night. At least I don't have to do that any more. Although," I added gloomily, "I would actually prefer that to her snoring and talking, but I'd have to wait until Derrick went to bed and then get up the minute he came down. And knowing him he'd probably sit up talking at me all night and *never* go to bed."

"Well at least we're getting used to the strawberry smell," said Ryan. "I've almost stopped noticing it."

"And me and Daisy think it's nice," added Claire.

"Ohhhh!" I buried my head in my hands.

"Look," said Boy Dave impatiently. "It's easy. We'll find a way of terrorizing him until he goes home."

Ryan looked interested. "What sort of terror were you thinking?"

"Well, we could say Jordan's house is haunted and then haunt him – but, like, really horrifically, with fake blood and that."

I sighed. "I have thought about it – loads. It's just that all this poor auntie stuff makes it really hard."

"I can understand you feeling sorry for him," agreed Claire.

"I don't feel at all sorry for him!" I snapped. "I'm just scared of what Mum would do if she found out."

I was suddenly interrupted by a different sort of loud snap from the corner of the barn. "Oh." Ryan looked excited. "That's the fourth one this week. It's my mousetrap," he explained. "It catches them alive so I can. . ." He saw the expressions on our faces. "Look at them," he finished lamely.

Ryan isn't exactly well known for being humane when it comes to the interests of science.

His mousetrap was made of a plastic bottle with the top cut off. From what I could gather, as soon as the mouse went in, a sort of guillotine dropped over the front, blocking its escape.

"I've found these help." Ryan wriggled on a pair of leather gloves. "They don't half bite."

Given that their fate was to have Ryan "look at them", I didn't blame them.

Sliding off the guillotine front, Ryan flipped the bottle up and swiftly put his gloved hand over the top of it. "This is the enclosure." He was heading for what looked like an old rabbit hutch – only smaller. "They used to store cheese in these things in the old days to keep mice out. Funny that, when you think about it."

I bent down and peered through the wire mesh. "It's very crowded. Don't you think it's a bit cruel?

There must be about ten layers of them piled up in there."

Ryan looked surprised. "I was thinking they all looked quite cosy. Anyway, I'm going to build them a run when I get time, with interesting challenges for them to overcome."

"Wouldn't it be easier to just let them go?" asked Claire, eyeing the sweaty box of fur pityingly. "That way you could . . . well. . ."

"Have the pleasure of catching them again," finished Daisy enthusiastically.

"It's kind of you to think of it," said Ryan, "but there's plenty out there."

"Pity Derrick isn't scared of mice," I said, as we let loose the last of the lucky fifty per cent of mice that Ryan had finally agreed to us liberating. "I could just put a load in his bed."

Ryan, who was watching cat-like as the last mouse disappeared into the wall, said thoughtfully, "How do you know he isn't?"

His eyes gleamed suddenly behind his glasses. "Yeah . . . I mean how do you know *what* would or wouldn't terrify him?"

It was certainly food for thought.

Actually scrap the "food". Whatever was going to terrify him, it certainly wasn't that.

Or so I thought. But we get to that later.

Sixteen

When I got home for tea I was starving, but at the sound of Derrick's familiar drone coming from the living room, I stopped. It was getting to the point where I had to use all my will power just to sit down at the same table with him. It was only a matter of time before I leapt up and smashed something over his head just to shut him up.

Taking a deep breath, I pushed open the door. At least it looked like proper food at last – chicken drumsticks and chips.

"The bed is harder than I'm used to," Derrick was saying. "I tend to feel where a mattress is concerned it really is worth investing in good quality. . ."

Dad, who was gripping his drumstick so tightly it was like he was going to punch someone with it, bit down accidentally on the bone. He swore loudly.

There was a bit of a silence. Mum would normally have told him off, but it was like she had no spirit left. Joanna said "Dad!" in a feeble-sounding voice, and Dulcie, who was trying to block Derrick out with her crossword, said, "Invalid woman, weedy conclusion, six letters."

Derrick sighed to show we'd interrupted him and began again; this time, seeing as I had arrived, it was about how parents should bring their children up knowing how to behave in "polite society".

I gazed at the faces round the table. The shipwrecked look from the restaurant hadn't faded at all. And there was still over one and a half months to go. We'd never make it.

"Uncle Derrick," I said in a tactful sort of voice, "I hope you don't mind me saying, but you don't seem to be very upset about poor dear Auntie . . . sorry, what was your wife's name again?"

I would say there was a bit of a silence, but it was worse than that. Dad's drumstick froze halfway to his mouth. Joanna's mouth dropped open so fast some food fell out. Dulcie carried on looking at her crossword, but like she wasn't seeing it at all, and Mum sat back in her chair as if someone had shoved her there.

"Jordan!" she gasped.

In fact, the only person who didn't seem particularly bothered was Derrick.

"Maureen," he told me calmly. "Aye, well, can't be helped."

Dad made a sort of choking noise. "Good for you, mate."

"In some ways –" Derrick munched thoughtfully on a mouthful of chips "– it might be for the best. I mean, I can do for myself well enough, although without Maureen the housework does tend to pile up and. . ."

"Yes," I interrupted hastily. "There's no need to start dron . . . going into detail. What I mean is, don't you think you would be so much happier at home with your . . . memories. I mean, it can't be much fun for you coming to a strange and hostile place and. . ."

"Jordan!" Mum croaked again.

Derrick looked down sadly at his empty plate. "Is there any more?"

"I . . . no," said Mum weakly.

Derrick sighed and shook his head. "I don't know why she had to go in the first place. If you ask me it was a lot of unnecessary fuss and expense. But as so often happens with women I didn't get much of a say in it. . ."

Dad, who looked as if he might like to agree on that one, chomped thoughtfully, but Mum looked horrified.

"And I suppose she'll be getting some peace and quiet now," continued Derrick mournfully. "Although I can't see why a few renovations and having a new kitchen fitted should cause quite so much fuss. And I did say to Maureen that we would eat out on

Christmas day, but for some reason she decided she couldn't stand that. . ."

"Having a new kitchen fitted, are you?" asked Dad. For the first time ever he looked a bit interested in something Derrick had said. He likes buildery-type conversations.

"Aye." Derrick sighed heavily. "We're having a new kitchen fitted. That was the cause of all this fuss in the first place. Maureen decided she just couldn't cope."

Mum's eyes were like saucers. "She . . . took her own life?" she breathed.

"Nooo." Derrick looked vaguely surprised. "She took a winter cruise with her sister Janet. I thought Janet told you. It was only because you invited me here that I agreed to her going in the first place. I mean, who was going to do for me at Christmas otherwise?"

What followed this was absolute dead silence.

"That. . ." said Mum. I got the feeling that Janet was being mentally obliterated from the Christmas list – but only because she wasn't there to be obliterated in person. "Isn't exactly the story I got."

Then a strange thing happened. Dad threw his head back and laughed until the tears ran down his cheeks.

*

"The trouble is, they feel as if they can't go back on it now," I told Boy Dave and Ryan at break the next day. "Plus Dad thinks it's hilarious. I whispered to him, wasn't it great that we could get rid of Derrick now, but he just said, 'Poor old sod, she faked her own death just to get away from him.' And burst out laughing again. He went down the pub –" I nodded at Boy Dave "– to tell your dad all about it."

"But that's great," said Boy Dave. "Not telling my dad, I mean. We can *definitely* get rid of Derrick now."

"And I know a brilliant way of doing it so that no one would know it was you," said Ryan.

"I don't think we should inject him with chemicals or anything," I said nervously.

"No, no. That was just . . . well. As you know," Ryan swept on hastily, as me and Boy Dave tried to remember any occasions when we might have felt a sneaky pin prick, "psychology is another of my interests, and I think the best way to do this is to use a type of psychological warfare. First we need to find out if your uncle has any phobias."

"You mean like a fear of heights?"

"Well, not heights necessarily. Any phobia. It was Boy Dave saying about terrifying him with ghosts that made me think about it. And then you said about the mice. . ."

Boy Dave looked pleased, but I was starting to get

confused. "You mean like fear of ghosts or fear of mice? Or ghost mice? Or . . . high-up ghosts? Or high up ghost mice. OH wait I get it. . ."

Ryan interrupted impatiently. "Forget ghosts. We're talking about his own special worst nightmare. Say your Uncle Derrick had a phobia about snakes, right? We would just arrange for him to keep 'accidentally' encountering them everywhere he went. Within days he'd be a gibbering wreck and have to flee."

"Hmm, it's a good idea, but it might be a bit hard getting hold of all the snakes."

"It could be a mixture of fake and live ones," pointed out Boy Dave.

"And," agreed Ryan, "one snake could make several appearances."

"But what if his phobia turned out not to be snakes?"

"Well, we'll do the same thing, only with that," said Ryan impatiently. "All you have to do is find out which terror it is."

Seventeen

Researching Derrick's phobias turned out to be easier said than done. Even if I did manage to get a member of my family out of earshot of Derrick, it was really difficult to suddenly bring it up out of the blue. Especially as just the mention of him plunged everyone into instant gloom. As for asking Derrick himself, it was kind of the same problem. If I tried to mention it quietly, he talked over me and I couldn't shout because it would have been a dead giveaway.

The best chance came on Thursday afternoon. It was Bonfire Night and Dad had gone up to The Black Horse to "help" set up their midnight river display. Derrick had gone to the toilet.

"There's a girl at our school who's got a phobia about heights," I said casually. "I was just wondering if anyone else round here had a phobia of any kind."

Joanna said, "I've got a phobia about you."

"I mean –" I paused as if thinking "– take Uncle Derrick, for instance. I wonder if he's got any particular phobias. Just plucking someone out of the air," I said hastily. "As an example."

Mum shot me a suspicious look. "What are you up—"

Luckily Dulcie interrupted her. "I knew a man who was phobic about the colour green. Or so I was told afterwards." She put on her remembering face. "I wore my best green dress to his dinner party. It was like something out of Edgar Allen Poe. With a look of white-faced terror he rose to his feet and pointed a quivering finger at me, but the fear had rendered him speechless."

Surprisingly for her, Joanna was unusually understanding. "That is just so embarrassing. There's nothing worse than a fashion faux pas."

"No," agreed Dulcie, eyeing her thoughtfully. Joanna was looking especially "from beyond the grave" that day. "Unless, of course, one counts world poverty and genocide. The poor man had to be helped from the room."

"And you had to leave in disgrace?" said Joanna sympathetically.

"Nonsense. I allowed myself to be shown to my seat and ate dinner as if nothing had happened. I mean, really! A phobia of green!"

I sat back and stuck my hands in my pockets thoughtfully. Even just rendering Derrick speechless would be a start. I tried to remember if he'd had any funny reactions to colours lately.

*

But by that evening I was feeling less hopeful.

"It's really difficult," I told Boy Dave and Ryan. Mum and Shelly (Boy Dave's mum) had gone up The Black Horse and we were on our way to the school display on the field. Not that the fireworks looked like being up to much. It had been murky and overcast all day and was already starting to drizzle. "Even if they did know Derrick's darkest fears, they're not likely to tell me."

"Hmm," said Ryan. "Maybe you could actually try a few on him and see what his reaction was. I mean, let's say you had a mouse. You could show it to him and if he screamed and shook with terror you'd know that was the one."

"It would be good if it did turn out to be mice," I told him. "Something like heights would be really difficult."

"Yeah," agreed Boy Dave. "It would be really hard getting him to high places without him realizing."

We'd reached the top field by now. It was in darkness apart from the outlines of little groups huddled together and sprinkled dots of torchlight. A few shadowy figures were scurrying around the bonfire trying to light it.

We wandered down to the edge of the safety tape looking out for Claire and Daisy, but it was impossible to see who anyone was. Down by the stream more dark figures were scurrying – setting up the fireworks.

In the distance, there was the occasional series of dull flashes, but that was all. It didn't have the atmosphere of a proper fireworks night at all.

About ten minutes later, the rain came crashing down. The bonfire, which had only a few moments before had sparked feebly into life, died and everyone charged up the field in search of cover. Already the field was turning to a mush of slippery mud.

"Arrgh, yuck!" Boy Dave spat the water out of his mouth. "What a waste of time."

"It's the worst one I can ever remember," I agreed. We were crushed with a whole crowd of other people into the hut at the top of the field.

"Remember, remember the fifth of November," said Boy Dave depressingly. "When it blooming chucked it down."

Ryan took off his streaming glasses and stared short-sightedly up at the sky.

"They'll have to cancel it now," he said cheerfully. "This won't let up for ages."

From where we were standing there was nothing to be cheerful about.

"But don't you see? This is great!" Ryan popped his glasses back on. "Think about it – by Saturday they'll all be gagging for a decent fireworks display."

Poppy Lockhart must have used unusual stealth for such a round person to get this close, but suddenly an eager moony face appeared beside Boy Dave.

"Hi, David." She's wanted Boy Dave to go out with her since year seven.

He glared at her. "Bog off, Poopy."

"What were you talking about?" Emma Chichester shoved her mousy pink nose in beside Poppy's.

"None of your bu—"

"The fireworks display this Saturday," interrupted Ryan. "I've heard it's going to be a real extravaganza. It's only three pounds to get in as well."

And so it began.

Eighteen

Literally overnight we become obsessed with the display. Even if we saw a kid just walking down the street, we crept up and slipped them a flyer.

We'd made them as soon as we got back, drenched, that night. They just said there would be a fireworks extravaganza on the school field that Saturday with soup and rolls and that entry was three pounds. With any luck people would think it was to make up for the school one and not ask too many questions. And just to be on the safe side, we only gave them out to kids. By Friday afternoon nearly everyone we'd handed fliers to had said they were coming.

On the way home that afternoon we did some exciting sums in our heads. If it all went well, we'd make about £150 on the gate alone. And if everyone bought soup it could go up to as much as £250. We'd never had that much money in one hit before in our lives.

"And we don't need to actually spend a whole thirty quid each on presents either," said Boy Dave.

"If we're careful we could get it down to half that and no one would notice."

But on the village green we hit a blip. We were halfway across when we saw Louse and Xathian sitting on the bench by the duck pond.

"Oi, what's this about a firework thing?" yelled Xathian.

We ignored them but they caught us up at the edge of the green.

"Whose show is this?" demanded Xathian. "It's not the school's because I checked."

We tried to blank our faces, but it wasn't easy. There we were, a day away from victory, and now Creep Features was trying to ruin it.

"Isn't it?" Ryan shrugged. "We don't really know. Some woman asked us to give them out."

Xathian and Louse exchanged sly glances.

"Oh," said Xathian in a normal-sounding voice. "I see. Thank you for explaining that."

He jerked his head at Louse and they wandered back. As we watched them go, I think we were all agreed on one thing – Xathian being normal was the creepiest he'd ever been.

We spent the rest of the afternoon looking up phobias on the internet and drinking fizzy orange in Boy Dave's den.

The ones we hoped Derrick didn't have were:

* Flying
* Heights
* Bridges
* Dentists
* Open spaces
* Small spaces

More hopeful were:

* Mice
* Birds
* Spiders
* Snakes
* Buttons
* And various colours

But even though reading about the phobias was quite interesting, it was hard to put Xathian completely out of our minds. We just had to hope he didn't tell his dad and that Harold didn't somehow try and put a stop to it. I mean, Harold might be a blood-sucking creature of the night, but he was also a very snobby grown-up and we didn't trust Xathian not to try and wreck everything just out of spite.

"They can't know it's us that organized it, though," said Boy Dave. He sort of said this out of the blue, but we'd all been thinking about it. "I mean, for all they know it's just a . . . well wisher."

"Yeah," I told him. "Then again, there's been quite a lot of stuff in our lives that we thought they couldn't possibly be sure was us, remember?"

"Look on the bright side," said Ryan. "The only way they'll know it's us is when we actually light the fireworks, and by then it'll be too late."

Nineteen

The whole next day I felt nervous, but by lunchtime I started to relax. Dad was working down at the school, but by the time the extravaganza started he and Big Dave would be long gone. I'd already told Mum I was having tea at Ryan's. Me and Boy Dave had arranged to meet him at his straight after lunch to pick up the fireworks and I was keen to get my lunch down and be off.

"It's like everything is just what we believe," said Joanna meaningfully. "Like, gravity only works because we *think* it does. Xathian says that with the right mindset anything is possible. . ."

"A boil the size of a medium-sized gold ball," droned Derrick. "Absolutely filled with pus. . ."

"I mean, like, think about it? Why can't we fly? What if we just shut our eyes and spread out our arms and. . ."

"Gravity," interrupted Dulcie. "As you said, dear."

"Joanna," said Mum sternly. "A word of advice – if you must fly, start low."

"Or high," I suggested. "Just believe, that's what I

say. Right." I gulped down my last mouthful. "I'm off."

I bolted speedily for the hall and shoved my trainers on. This was great! No ominous knock at the door. No PC White or Harold asking awkward questions. Two hundred and fifty pounds! My heart beat faster – we'd be rich! We'd have to be sensible, obviously. I mean, there was no point just spending it all. . .

A knock sounded at the door. I froze.

Everyone was still in the living room. I strained my ears for the sound of someone coming to answer but there was nothing – just Derrick droning on.

Seconds ticked by.

They couldn't have heard – either that or they just thought it was me leaving. Stealthily I crept over on my knees and pulled up the letter box.

It was like Dulcie's man with the phobia. At the sight of the black polo neck outside, the colour drained from my face.

I tried to squash down the panic. All I had to do was sit tight until Harold realized we were all out and went away. Just have to hope he didn't flap up and get through a window or something. Nervously I peered back through the letter box. With any luck he'd . . . URGHH! A pair of green-tinted, puffy, evil little eyes were staring right back.

"Is that you, Mrs Smith?" The creepy whine came dangerously loudly through the letter box.

"Er . . . ye-es." (Oh wow, he thought I was Mum.)

"Are you going to open the door?"

Arghhh, what was that rule again? A vampire can only come into your house if you invite him.

"No way! I mean . . . I'm . . . not we-ell."

"Oh dear." Harold's eyes pressed closer. I pressed mine closer too, in case he saw round the gaps. "Is there anything I can do?"

Sooo not! Must remember to do the Mum voice, though.

"No, thank you. I . . . I just need to be on my own right now. I have a very catching disease and—"

"Jordan! Who's that at the door?" The real Mum voice sounded like the bell of doom behind me.

"No o-one. Er, I mean, no one."

Mum stomped crossly past me and Harold almost fell into our hall.

"Oh, you're . . . better." He stared up at her through his little green glasses.

"Mum!" I cried desperately. "You need to rest."

Mum ignored me.

"You're from next door, aren't you?" she said nicely.

"Don't invite him in!" I cried, even more desperately.

"Come in," said Mum.

Surprisingly, instead of baring his fangs in triumph,

Harold dithered rudely like he had when Dad offered him the tea.

"Well . . . I only came round to give you this."

Mum looked down at the flyer he'd handed her and her face darkened. This was it. My heart thumped. Xathian had told him everything. That weird pathetic little creep had managed to wreck it all at the last minute. I could just hear it – any second now – the phone call to Dad, the phone call to the school, the phone call to Boy Dave's mum and dad, the grounding, the threats, the—

"So you're producing the Christmas village show this year?" Mum looked up. "Well, it'll make a change from a panto, I suppose."

"It's to be a version of a sort of modern-day nativity," said Harold proudly. "Using the nativity as a metaphor for. . ."

But by then I was through the garden gate and running.

Twenty

Normally the unveiling of an invention takes place in Ryan's mum's barn but, as he explained, there had been a few problems involving the pagan hens and a bit of gunpowder. Instead we followed Ryan down the twisty, overgrown path to his "laboratory".

"When you said three –" Boy Dave peered nervously into the cobwebby, burned-smelling shed "– I thought you meant. . ."

"That's what I was trying to tell you," said Ryan proudly. "These are no ordinary fireworks."

He could say that again. They were more like cardboard nuclear warheads.

"Where did you get the tubes?" I asked.

Ryan looked pleased. He likes explaining his inventions. "They were left over from one of my mum's sculptures. Originally they were used for paper on printing presses. Basically it's the same as creating, say, a rocket, but in a much larger cylinder."

I did a quick calculation. Just one of the tubes was about five normal rockets round – with maybe an extra one in the middle – and about three, maybe four rockets high. Five times four was . . . oh wow! Just one of Ryan's fireworks was over twenty times more powerful than a normal rocket.

"I. . ." I blinked nervously, "don't want to be the one to ask, but isn't that a bit dangerous? I mean, these look way more than level four. What if they just fall out of the sky?"

Ryan tutted like I'd said something stupid. "It's not going to be in the sky. The main structure will stay on the ground, obviously."

Boy Dave frowned. "Er, I'm probably missing something here, but I don't see how that would be any safer."

"Look!" Ryan glared at us. "*IF* you don't mind my saying so – who is the one out of all of us who understands the most about chemistry?"

"You are," we mumbled, "but. . ."

"Do you really think," he said haughtily, "that I would be such an idiot as to simply . . . fill one of these tubes up with gunpowder and put a fuse on it?"

"Well didn't you?" I asked nicely.

"Of course not. That would just be a kind of bomb. These are highly sophisticated constructions. These tubes," Ryan waved an arm, "contain many special chemical effects which will be spectacular to the eye of the beholder."

Boy Dave was still frowning. "How do you know they won't just explode?"

Ryan looked surprised. "Of course they're going to explode. They're fireworks."

"I think what he means," I explained, "is explode in a really dangerous way."

"Ahh." Ryan held up a finger. "Well you see, whereas with normal fireworks you would run a fuse between them and they would go off at, say, two-second intervals, my fireworks are a self-contained sequence of different exciting effects. The beauty of it is that you can set all three going at once. It will be like watching an entire fireworks display all at the same time!"

"And the danger bit?" I reminded him.

"Well, there isn't really any as such. The different events are completely self-contained except for timed fuses linking them together – different substances burn at different rates. I mean, take a rook scarer; the fuse burns at six inches per hour. Then again a tube of black powder would burn the same distance in minutes depending how thick it was. Then there's manufacturer's putty, which does one centimetre per second, but that's restricted category so I had to improvise. The point being that the overall effect is unpredictable to the audience, but really isn't any more dangerous than an ordinary fireworks display." He stopped breathlessly. "Does that clarify the situation?"

Me and Boy Dave looked at each other. From what we could gather the main difference between Ryan's fireworks and normal ones was that his were a bit more confusing to watch. Given that Ryan had invented them this wasn't really surprising.

Apart from a sudden deep fear of naked flames, we got the fireworks down to the school field quite easily. We'd taken the back route through the woods just in case, but with any luck mine and Boy Dave's dads had finished at the gym by now. Even if they hadn't they couldn't see the field from where they were anyway.

The tape was still up from Thursday's display so all we had to do was jam the fireworks into the mud where the others had been.

We waited for Claire and Daisy in a tree on the other side of the stream. Dusk had fallen and it was a relief when two dark shapes finally appeared at the top of the field. They were loaded up with bags and were carrying one of those small, round barbecues on legs.

"We've managed to pinch a load of cups and serviettes as well," said Daisy. "We're going to charge two pounds a cup and fifty pence for bread. We've got enough here for about fifty. How many are you expecting?"

"We've kind of lost track," I told her, "but it's loads."

If I'm being honest, I sounded more confident than I felt. It was so quiet and empty out there on the field it was hard to imagine it suddenly filling up with people.

"Try and make sure you only give them small portions," said Boy Dave, who didn't seem to be sharing any of my worries. "That way they'll need seconds."

It was now five o' clock and we were starting to get nervous. Claire and Daisy had lit the barbecue and the soup was bubbling. There was half an hour left now and the night had turned out perfect – clear and cold. There was nothing left to do but wait.

We sat down by the stream on the other side of the field and ate a supper of bread and tomato soup. The minutes ticked by slowly. In the darkness the three enormous tubes were as still as gravestones. Behind us the branches creaked quietly in the woods, and far off across the fields an owl hooted.

I imagined her, wings spread wide, her shadow falling over her prey. It would freeze, pretending to be dead – or nothing – like a clod of earth. But she would know. In the quiet of the night she would hear its heart still beating. And she would come then, swooping down until she was gliding low, a foot or so above the ground. At exactly the right moment she would stretch out her talons and take him.

I wondered if there were any owls out there in the woods listening to my heart. If there were they would have jumped as much as I did as Ryan let out a sudden yell. "People!"

He was right. As if from nowhere a raggedy line of torchlight had appeared, straggling out across the top of the field.

Twenty-one

It was the weirdest thing I'd ever known. My pockets were heavy with money and people kept handing me more.

"Three pounds, please," Boy Dave was saying. "Three pounds."

I started to wonder if I would wake up. There we were standing either side of the field entrance and as people walked past they were just handing us money.

Well, not quite like a dream.

"Why should I give it to you?" Conner eyeballed me in the torchlight. "You'll just put it in your pocket."

"Yes," I told him nicely. "That's where I'm keeping it."

He scowled down the field. "This is a wind-up."

"Tell you what," said Boy Dave. "You give me your money, then go down and look by the stream. If there aren't any fireworks I'll give you your. . ."

I didn't hear the next bit. From the corner of my eye I'd suddenly become worryingly aware of two dark figures making their way up the steps from the lower yard.

The headmistress of our school is Miss Stormberry. She's stout, and wears old-fashioned suits with baggy brown tights. Her accent is almost as posh as Dulcie's and she has a very noticeable strutting sort of walk. As for the other, I'd have known that marching stride anywhere. Mr Jefferson! Sadist and monster of the P.E. department, ex-army sergeant major maniac.

Forgetting the queue, I grabbed Boy Dave and dragged him running across the field.

"What are you doing?" he yelled crossly, trying to break away. "What about the money?"

"It's Jefferson!" I panted. "And I think the other one is the headmistress."

I'd kind of expected that as soon as we'd warned the others we'd all run away. But even before we'd gasped out the bad news to Ryan, he'd ducked under the tape and pelted down the grass towards the pillars.

"Quickly!" he yelled over his shoulder. "Before they can stop us."

For a second, Boy Dave's eyes met mine. It was a desperate look and I knew exactly what he was thinking. Our pockets were full of other people's money. If we backed out now we'd be lynched at school on Monday. Either that or we'd have to give it all back. Whichever one, it didn't bear thinking about.

Within seconds we were hurtling down the field after Ryan.

"What do we do?" I gasped as we stumbled to a halt in front of the fireworks.

"Light that little string." Ryan pointed his torch at the ground. "Then run like the wind."

The string lit surprisingly easily – almost as soon as I held the match to it. For a moment I stared transfixed as the small spark fizzed into life; then, heart banging, I skidded upright again and pelted away across the grass.

A crowd had started to gather interestedly on the other side of the safety tape and we had to jostle ourselves a space. In the expectant hush that fell, the tubes were like three dark, ancient monuments that had lain undiscovered for thousands of years and would put a curse on all those who found them.

I cast a nervous glance over my shoulder. Jefferson and the headmistress had reached the edge of the crowd.

"Why aren't they working?" hissed Boy Dave desperately.

"They will," Ryan hissed back. "I mixed a few substances together to make the fuses so I can't be sure of the exact times before they reach the first lot of propellants."

Unfortunately there wasn't the same confusion

about the exact time Jefferson and the headmistress would take to reach us.

"Just what is going on here?" demanded a voice. The headmistress was bustling her way through the last of the throng. Beside her marched Jefferson, mowing down anyone who got in his way. His eyes, which had been swivelling from side to side like a mad axe man, went suddenly still like glass. He leant forward and peered towards the stream.

"You will go and take those contraptions down with immediate effect," he told us in a surprisingly normal voice. "As of now they is the property of me. As for youse three, come Monday morning you is also going to be the property of me. And as such you is going to wish you 'ad never been born."

We fidgeted nervously.

"NOW!" he bellowed.

There was a small silence.

"We can't," mumbled Ryan. "They're lit."

Longer silence.

"They is lit," echoed Jefferson heavily.

For a moment me, Boy Dave, Ryan, Jefferson and the headmistress all stared into the darkness at the spectacular lack of explosion. Meanwhile, the crowd behind us began to mutter impatiently.

"This is most unsafe!" The headmistress blinked worriedly. "We must clear the area."

The effect was that Jefferson opened his mouth to

115

shout and a hideous noise came out. Not the usual hideous noise, though.

"ARRAGHARRAGHARRAGHA."

It took a while for us to realize that the noise wasn't Jefferson at all and that it was coming from further along the safety string.

As near to the front as they had managed to get were Xathian and Louse complete with battery amp. Xathian was thrashing wildly at his guitar while behind him Louse was pounding proudly away at a wobbly drum kit, trying not to fall off the stool.

No wonder they never dobbed us in. They most likely had all sorts of great images of being the amazing, weird stars of the show. With fireworks going off behind them they could pretend to be rock stars.

And weren't they loving it! As if from nowhere, their following of the death pandas had appeared. Worse still, Joanna, wearing a black cape and hood (which I think might have been Dulcie's rain things), seemed to be doing backing vocals.

"ARRAGHARRAGHADEATHVAMPIRE," roared Xathain.

"Oooooooooaaaaaaahhhh," howled Joanna.

CRASH, THUMP went Louse.

"ARRAGGHHAAMOONFEAST."

"Aaaaaaaooooooohhhhhh."

SMASH, SMASH, SMASH.

116

I think it must have been more from instinct than actual choice, but the whole crowd turned to look. This was terrible. Not only did it seem like we hadn't got any fireworks, but everyone would think this was our fault as well. And if the youth club "gig" was anything to go by, we just had to pray that Werewolf and his gang weren't about.

Luckily (I mean luckily at the time, although not so much later on), Xathian's glory didn't last long.

In the same way that instinct had made the crowd all turn round at the sound of a loud noise, they all turned back again. One of Ryan's fuses had finally hit its target.

Twenty-two

There was a deafening bang, followed by a huge whoosh, and the sky above the trees turned lime green. "Ooooh," went the crowd wonderingly. Ryan grinned at us, his face eerie in the green light. He tried to yell something but there was another loud whoosh. When I say "whoosh", I mean a sound like you'd imagine the air being sucked out of space to make a black hole would make. It was like a great wind howling in through one ear and blasting your brains out of the other.

With an ear-splitting bang, an enormous red fireball spurted out of the top of the second tube and hurtled skywards. It exploded into a shower of red glowing blobs, splattering the trees on the bank like a weird disease. Meanwhile the first one let off a huge explosion, and a football-sized blue fireball shot into the air. There was a sound a bit like a steam train and the sky was filled with blobby blue rain.

The third firework remained ominously silent.

At first the headmistress and Jefferson had been too distracted to do anything, but when the blue rain started to fall they sprung suddenly into life.

"ARRAGHARRAGARAGHH," went Xathian. "ARRGGAGHHlllmgerroff!"

Jefferson yanked the radio mike off his ears. "FALL BACK," he yelled into it. "TROOP MOVE OUT!"

The headmistress was trying to herd people away but they kept swerving and coming back. No wonder Jefferson thought we were under fire, though. Down by the stream it was like a war zone. Bangs and whooshes were followed by fireball after fireball, and what sounded like machine-gun volleys. The sky was changing colour so fast it was like someone pressing a remote.

I rubbed my streaming eyes and started to feel as if the war zone was actually inside my head. The air was filled with the smell of burning gunpowder and the thick black smoke that had been rolling steadily towards us had finally made it past the tape. I could still just about make out the coloured sky, but on the ground you couldn't see anything at all.

I wasn't the only one who was feeling the effects. Once the smoke hit, the crowd started to thin out fast. I grabbed Boy Dave and tried to shout to him that maybe we should back up a bit too, but the smoke got in my lungs.

The next thing I knew, Boy Dave had grabbed me and Ryan and was dragging us, coughing our guts out, towards the clear air at the top of the field.

It was about then that the third firework went off.

Basically it was like when I poured Derrick's drink on Dulcie's newspaper, but multiplied by a hundred. A huge flame shot into the air, there was a deafening volley of bangs, and the whole thing basically just exploded. By now we were all running for our lives.

"Claire!" I looked back wildly. "Daisy!"

But the barbecue was deserted. We stared down the field but it was more or less in darkness. After the first massive explosion, the third firework seemed to have burned itself out. Either that or toppled into the stream. From what we could see, only the first one was still popping off a few feeble sparks.

"What're all those blobs on the trees?" I rasped. My throat felt like I'd been swallowing razor blades.

Ryan tried to polish his sooty glasses on the sleeve of his jumper.

"I expect it's the magnesium." He sounded like something out of a cowboy film. "It goes red when. . ."

It was then we heard the sirens.

Twenty-three

That Monday morning mine and Boy Dave's walk to school was about the most depressing it'd ever been. On Sunday there had been two minutes' silence – lest we forget. And then there had been unbearable silence of the rest of the day from our families (bar Derrick, obviously) and a whole load of stuff there was no chance of ever forgetting.

"I suppose the fireman came to yours as well," said Boy Dave eventually.

I nodded without bothering to look up.

"And you told them we bought the fireworks from a stall in Brighton like we agreed?"

"Yes, but they don't believe me. They just can't think where else they could have come from."

"I suppose you're grounded as well."

"For ever," I told him dully. "The worst thing is that for the first time in our whole lives I think we might even deserve it. Did the fire officer make you look at the photos of firework injuries?"

"Yeah." Boy Dave swallowed. "And I couldn't help

thinking that if that's what normal fireworks can do to people. . ."

He didn't need to say any more. Someone could have been really badly hurt, or even killed, because of us. And that was that. No way round it. It wasn't our "safety procedures" that had kept everyone safe that night, it was just sheer luck.

The thought of what could have happened was like a cold, grey jelly that had settled in the pit of my stomach and wouldn't go away. Even in my sleep.

We had stopped by the village pond. Jagged pieces of thin ice floated on its surface. It didn't matter any more that the weather was turning colder and that our very own ice rink might soon be frozen over. Or that in three weeks' time the lighting up of the main street would mean the official start of Christmas. The village could be lit up like a galaxy for all it would mean to us.

"It's the worst grounding I've ever had," I moaned. We had begun the trudge up the hill towards the school. "I can't even hide in my room because Joanna's totally taken it over. Having to sit downstairs with Mum and Dad is terrible, but with Derrick there it's a nightmare. I feel as if I'm going mad."

"You'll be out of your mind soon," agreed Boy Dave gloomily.

"I have never. . ." Suddenly I felt like bursting into tears. "In my life felt so bad about anything. It's like

I feel too guilty to even look forward to Christmas. That and having Derrick there wrecking it anyway."

"They can't be serious about not letting us out at all for the whole holidays." Boy Dave kicked crossly at someone's dustbin. "It's inhuman."

"They are. I've tried to explain over and over again that we just had no idea it was all going to go like that, but they don't care."

"Mine think we were trying to blow up the school. With the amount of times we've been accused of it, I'm starting to think we might as well just go ahead and do it."

"Yeah, and knowing our luck the school would probably double in size instead."

"Oi!" Ryan, looking a bit puffed out and red in the face, caught up with us. "I've been calling you from right down the bottom!"

"Sorry," I said. "We were just talking about how well the extravaganza went."

Ryan fiddled with his glasses. "Well, obviously the extreme fireworks need a bit of tweaking."

We goggled. *"Tweaking!"*

"Well, all right then, toning down a bit. You've got to admit they're a lot better than normal ones, though."

Boy Dave gave him a pitying look. "But really they weren't so much fireworks as fireballs, weren't they?"

"And actual fire," I added. "With black smoke that almost choked us to death."

Ryan looked a bit hurt. "We've still got the money, haven't we?"

"Some," I told him gloomily. "Most of it fell out all over the school field in the blackout. We'll have to go up there and try and find it at break."

"If everyone else hasn't found it already," said Boy Dave depressingly. "And it's not as if we'll actually be able to go anywhere and spend it, is it?"

Ryan blinked and then carried on walking with his head down like we weren't there.

"Hey." I nudged him. "We're sorry. We didn't mean to be harsh."

"It's just that we got into really bad trouble," explained Boy Dave. "And I expect your mum's already forgotten all about it." He was trying to be nice but this last bit came out really bitter.

"More or less," admitted Ryan. "I think I was grounded after the fire officer came round, and had my pocket money stopped and that sort of thing. But then she got into making her mushrooms again. And this morning she told me she hoped I was going to be sensible this year. I suppose when you're artistic time does go a bit funny."

"Your mum's a bit funny, more like," said Boy Dave.

"She completely peculiar," agreed Ryan. "But that's because she's artistic."

"Don't worry," I told him. "We're just jealous. We wish our families were a bit more artistic, that's all."

What Ryan said next took us by surprise.

"Well," he said seriously. "I know you get into trouble a lot more than me and you probably won't believe this, but I'm sometimes jealous of you as well. At least your mums and dads actually notice what you do."

"Only the bad stuff," I told him kindly.

"I guess. Anyway, the good news is that my new invention will be perfect with our ice rink."

By now we were making our way across the schoolyard. Even the school building seemed to be looming over us more darkly and sinisterly than ever before.

"You don't understand," said Boy Dave tonelessly. "We can't do the ice rink now. We can't do anything now."

Ryan's mouth dropped open like he was about to say something but then couldn't think what to say.

"We're grounded," I told him. "Really badly, long -term grounded."

"But you can't be. What about. . .?"

"Over with," I told him bitterly. "Well and truly over."

Twenty-four

That night our mums and dads had a special parent-teacher meeting with PC White. Even Ryan's mum had to go. There was an agreement reached. Our mums and dads had to agree to make sure we would never do anything wrong ever again. If they didn't agree the school would suspend us. PC White said that if anything like this happened again he would charge us. The only reason it wasn't worse is because our mums and dads managed to persuade them that we'd just been trying to make it up to everyone about Thursday's fireworks. And Ryan's mum saw a fairy perched on Miss Stormberry's shoulder and kept telling her to keep "quite still".

That week was the most terrible one we'd ever had.

As far as our dads were concerned, trying to blow up the school was one thing, but being forced to attend a special parent-teacher meeting was unforgivable. For me and Boy Dave it was the house equivalent of living on death row.

In my house, it was like we weren't even a family

any more. Joanna had decided that the fireworks had been some kind of huge plot to destroy her, the Vampire Death Squad and all their followers.

"You could have *killed* us all!" she said for the millionth time over dinner that Wednesday.

"WE DIDN'T EVEN WANT YOU THERE!" I exploded finally. "You were the ones who gate-crashed our display. And anyway I'm surprised you're so worried about being killed seeing as you all think you're vampires and were-things and basically love the idea of being dead already!" There was silence except for me panting furiously. Dad and Mum stared at me with white faces and Joanna clutched her heart like I'd jammed a stake into it.

Derrick looked smug and drew in a big breath. He was obviously preparing for an epic rant but Dulcie said, "Well of course in the war lethal explosions were a way of life. Everyone just got on with it and managed to keep their hysteria to themselves. But then that's part of being British, isn't it?" She raised her head from her crossword and looked sternly at Derrick over her glasses. "Even the Scots. Just shutting up and getting on with it without moaning is the best foot forward so to speak? Don't you agree, Derrick?"

"Aye, well," began Derrick. "Then again, one must speak out against yobs who. . ."

Dad shoved his chair back. "I'm going down the pub."

I stared miserably at his half-eaten steak. Mum had made it for him specially, with the sauce that he really likes.

"And *I'm* going round Collette's!" said Joanna dramatically. "So I don't have to be in the same room as someone who's tried to murder me!"

"There's no need." Quietly I pushed back my own chair. "I'm going to my . . . the room. So you can all pretend I don't exist. And . . . and Dad can finish his steak," I whispered. "Please?"

As I made my way upstairs it was eerily quiet in the living room, but a few minutes later the front door slammed and a bit later it slammed again.

I lay on my bed and listened to the sounds of the house. The television was on, and I thought I heard the sound of the ironing board being clunked out. Derrick was droning as usual. I tried to shut him out, but it was difficult in the quiet. I supposed the living room door was open.

"I mean it's not something any parent would want to face up to. . ." His drone drifted up the stairs like poisoned gas. "But you should surely realize that ignoring a problem is like feeding compost to a plant. It will just continue to grow. I mean in my professional opinion as a GP I can tell you that your son obviously has delinquent tendencies. . ."

"Nonsense," came Dulcie's voice crossly. "Jordan is just naturally high-spirited – as a boy should be."

"And I don't want to be rude –" Mum sounded like she did actually, but was trying not to be "– but I'm not sure what problems we're actually talking about here."

"Aye, well." I could almost see Derrick rubbing his hands. "Take the whole sorry affair at the restaurant. I mean . . ." I couldn't believe it – he'd almost chuckled ". . . it was like flood, fire and famine. You're not trying to tell me that was normal behaviour? No, in my opinion. . ."

I knew Mum had gone red just from her tone of voice. "Jordan tried to flush his food down the toilet so that he wouldn't offend you!" she blurted out. "And the fire was nothing to do with him, as well you know. And as for famine! Dominic paid you back for the meal. . ." I curled my toes uncomfortably. I hadn't known Dad had done that. "And you've certainly made up for it, haven't you?" Mum carried on furiously. "Famine indeed! You've done nothing but eat since you arrived!"

I felt a small prickle of excitement. Go on! Do it! Throw him out!

But it wasn't Mum who threw him out; it was Dulcie. And not quite in the way I'd hoped.

"Derrick!" Dulcie used to be a headmistress and now she spoke in her best headmistress's voice. "I suggest that you either go upstairs to your very comfortable room that Angela has provided for you, or you go for a long walk. She needs peace and quiet. Now GO!"

Wow – glad she wasn't my headmistress.

There was the sound of fatness trudging up the stairs and then a soft click as Derrick's bedroom door closed. Ha ha, Dulcie had sent him to his room. Except that . . . I suddenly wished Dad were here. He would . . . well, I didn't really know what he would do, but he would do something. . .

Cautiously I creaked off my bed and tiptoed downstairs.

"Honestly." Mum was slumped on the sofa in front of the ironing board. "That man!"

Dulcie gave her a kindly look. "Angela dear! I imagine there's nothing worse than someone criticizing the way you look after your children when you're doing the very best you can."

Mum looked down at her lap and shook her head. When she didn't look up I knew she was crying. I tried to swallow away the lump that had suddenly knotted up inside my throat.

"Mum?"

I don't often cuddle my mum – all that kind of stopped when I was about eight – but without thinking I went over and put my arms round her. I laid my head on her shoulder and it was strange because it felt that as if for years I'd forgotten what she smelled like. In a kind of flood I suddenly remembered back to when she smelled better than anything in the whole world.

"I'm sorry," I said into her jumper. "I'm really sorry."

She pulled away suddenly and gave me an angry kiss.

"Sorry for being you?" She smiled at me.

I hung my head. "Sorry for doing all the stuff that made him upset you."

"No," said Mum firmly. "He chose to upset me because for some reason he enjoys it. And if he wasn't moaning about you, he'd be moaning about something else."

"Angela?" We were surprised to see Dulcie wobbling over to us with a small glass of her favourite brown yuck and a plate of biscuits. "You're tired, dear." She pushed the glass into Mum's hand. "It's Derrick, he's wearing you out. From the moment Maureen married him I knew it was a mistake. That man would try the patience of a saint. Mind you," she added, "Maureen's not much better. They probably deserve each other. Honestly, Angela, you'll have to tell him it's too much for you and send him home."

"Well, Dominic told me he's going to sort it out, but . . . I don't know." Mum shrugged helplessly. "And I mean I wouldn't know what to say. It's not as if he actually *does* anything. Apart from sit there and moan."

"And moan," I added.

"And eat us out of house and home," said Mum.

It must have been the stress, because we all burst out laughing.

In a way, even though Mum had been upset, I did feel better after that. On the other hand I was more determined than ever that Derrick had to go. The sooner the better. But how? Me and Boy Dave couldn't even leave our houses. And at school it was like people were watching us all the time. Even break times were bad. No one seemed to actually want to talk to us but that didn't stop them giving us funny looks and whispering when we went by.

That Friday lunchtime, me and Boy Dave were kicking a ball against the wall to one another when Ryan appeared out of nowhere. The ball nearly knocked his head off but he was too excited to notice.

"I've put your names down," he told us joyfully. "On the noticeboard."

We looked at him. If there was one thing we didn't need it was someone being cheerful around us.

"For extras in the village nativity?" Ryan said this like he was reminding us. "It said quite clearly 'everyone welcome' but no one's bothered. Apart from you," he added proudly.

We goggled. As if helping to get us the worst grounding we'd ever had wasn't bad enough, he'd decided to torture us with village activities as well.

"I've got it written down." He pulled his ragged notebook out of his pocket. "Rehearsals are on Saturday afternoon, and Tuesday and Thursday evenings instead of youth club. And some Sunday afternoons nearer the time."

He snapped the notebook shut again looking pleased. "I've got the forms ready for your parents to fill in."

"Why?" asked Boy Dave pitifully. "Why are you doing this to us?"

Ryan looked surprised. "I thought you'd be pleased."

"But doing the nativity will be terrible," I told him. "Don't you know who's in charge of it? Dad of the dead, that's who. Harold the snooty vampire."

"Well that's because he once had something in the West End," said Ryan. "All the village committees and whatnot think we're going to suddenly become the arts capital of England."

"Village of the vampire slaves, more like," I told him.

"Yeah," Boy Dave chipped in. "It's probably just a plot to get us all in one place so they can feast on us."

"They'll let the others out of their boxes," I agreed.

"Specially once they've got everyone gathered in one place."

Ryan blinked like we were particularly stupid lower life forms.

"I don't mean that you should actually *go* to the rehearsals." He sighed despairingly. "Don't you get it? The nativity is your very own first-class ticket to freedom!"

The next day I gloomily handed Mum an envelope. "They said I'm to give you this."

Mum was obviously struggling to read with Derrick there so in the end she took the letter out into the hall.

Meanwhile I fidgeted nervously at the table and waited. I wasn't at all curious about the letter. I was just worried that she might not fall for it. The evening before, Ryan had done one each for me and Boy Dave on official paper nicked from the school office.

Dear Mr and Mrs Smith,

Further to our discussions on Monday 9th November, I would like to make the following suggestion. While I appreciate that you are doing all you can to help Jordan understand how his actions make other people feel, his other teachers and I think that he would benefit from learning to be part of a group and mixing with other members of the village. In this way we think he might become less anti-social.

I have enclosed a form that I want to you sign allowing Jordan to take part in Harold Thorpe Jackson's village nativity. We all feel this would be an excellent learning experience and very character-building for Jordan. I realize that in the beginning this is something that Jordan might not want to do, but under the circumstances I think you should make him because it will be very good for him.

Please sign the enclosed forms and send them to the school.

Yours faithfully,

Miss Amelia Stormberry
Head Teacher

When Mum finally came back she looked prepared for battle. And for the battle that followed I should have got an Oscar.

Twenty-five

We had decided to go to a few rehearsals just so's we would know what was going on. But that was before we'd actually been to one. It was ten past seven on Thursday evening at the village hall and Harold had just appeared onstage from the shadows.

"Good evening, everybody." He gave a squinty smile. Behind the green of his glasses, his eyes swivelled. "Thank you all . . . for coming. I'm really very . . . excited . . . to be. . ." *Yeeach!* I'd never noticed it before but he writhed when he talked, like someone was dripping water down his back. "Working . . . with you all."

Me, Boy Dave and Ryan slid bravely into the furthest depths at the back. We'd put off actually going in until the last minute.

"As you all know, my vision for this . . . production . . . is as a sort of modern-day nativity play. I . . . intend that . . . each character will represent something more . . . symbolic."

"Excuse me!" said Mrs White. "I don't understand

what could be more symbolic than the baby Jesus?"

Harold squinted at her. "Indeed, but we are talking about the . . . modern day. . ."

"Nativities aren't modern day!" another hag from the Women's Institute interrupted loudly. "They represent an important historical. . ."

"What he's saying. . ." piped up Isaac from the other side of the hall. He sniffed into a large white hanky. "Excuse me, I think I've caught some sort of rare animal flu while I was up at the farm the other day. What he's saying is you can stick that story on to something else and make a point out of it for that other thing."

"But you can't just use it to make a point," said Mrs Bagnall, cheeks quivering. "It *is* the point."

This looked like it was going to go on for quite a while, but at that moment the vicar jumped up on to the stage and pointed out bad-temperedly that they only had the hall until nine so could everyone please just get on with it.

It was then that I noticed Mr Jolly. His real name is Izzy Gent, but we village kids call him Mr Jolly because of his Christmas decorations. The real Izzy Gent is a gloomy old man who spends most of the year on a bar stool down at the The Black Horse. Every year, though, on the first of December, it's like a fairy godmother turns him into Mr Jolly. Overnight every inch of his garden and the outside of his house is covered in lights and Christmas decorations. I mean, we're talking serious Christmas bling – six dwarf-sized moving santas in the window (at last count), massive inflatable sleigh and reindeer, other herd of lifelike reindeer with dip-down heads that pretend to eat grass, big inflatable snowman plus other little sorts; icicle lights everywhere, plus a big "Merry Christmas" on his roof like an American diner. There's loads more, but that's what I can remember off the top of my head. My mum said he's got lots of grandchildren, which is why he does it, but we all like it too. When Mr Jolly's lights go on it's like the official start to Christmas.

He was picking his nose and looking glum. He normally gets quite a big part in the village panto, which is usually a chaotic sort of event, where scenery falls down and you can hear voices inside the pantomime horse talking about the best way to grow marrows.

As for Harold's Nastyvity – the bit we saw was pretty boring. I mean, you'd at least have expected the baby Jesus to sprout wings and fly round like a bat. And Mary could suddenly have gone weird and showed her fangs to the three wise men, who would all have fled in terror with the baby in pursuit while weresheep devoured the shepherds. . .

So far as I could see, despite the pretended concern

from the Women's Institute witches, the only unusual bit would be when the boxes all burst open and Count Harold and the nest from next door plunged their fangs into everyone.

Our extras part went like this:

* "No room at the hostel"
* "Ahhhh"
* "Oooh" (with wonder)
* "Hallelujah!" (there were quite a few of those)

"Oh Joe!" Collette wrung her hands at Adam the butcher's boy. "What are we going to do?" She and Joanna have been hoping he'll ask them out since about year eight so I bet she was well pleased she was getting to do the show with him.

"Look to the heavens!" cried Harold excitedly.

I reached through the podge of Women's Institute and grabbed Ryan by the shoulder.

"Right, they've had their lot." (I copied Dad's expression.) "If I have to watch any more of it I'm going to puke."

We were so busy breathing in the frosty night air and looking wonderingly up at the moon (and enjoying freedom generally) that it wasn't until we were halfway down the road that we realized we'd been followed.

A small figure in a flat cap was trudging gloomily through the shadows behind us. Being an extra in Harold's show obviously wasn't Mr Jolly's idea of Christmas fun either.

As he turned into his gate it was hard to imagine that in a few weeks' time his drab little garden would be transformed into the most Christmassy place in the village.

"Doing the lights this year?" called Boy Dave. Mr Jolly straightened up and surveyed his garden anxiously.

"Got a new sleigh this year." He made it sound worrying. "Biggest one out. Import from the US. Larger than life size." He sighed nervously.

"Great," we told him. "Can't wait to see it."

"Where are you going to put it?" asked Boy Dave. "We actually said last year, didn't we?" He nodded to me and Ryan. "That we couldn't see how you could fit any more in."

"Big snowman and old Santa are going on the roof." Mr Jolly looked up apprehensively. "Little snowman next to the pond – moving the heron in – not really seasonal."

"He looked good with his Santa hat, though," I told him. I felt a bit sorry for the heron; after all, he'd taken part in the last few Christmases.

"Not seasonal," said Mr Jolly firmly.

"We could give you a hand putting the stuff on the

roof if you like," offered Boy Dave hopefully.

"Man with a ladder," said Mr Jolly, "what do they call them – window cleaner. He does that."

Ryan nodded his head back towards the village hall. "You didn't fancy the nativity, then?"

"No point me being there," said Mr Jolly sadly. "Not if they're not even going to see me."

Twenty-six

Feeling a bit sorry for him, we headed up towards Ryan's mum's barn.

"Cor," said Boy Dave, looking round. "Your mum's pagan mushrooms look like they've gone through a lawnmower."

"It's the pagan hens." Ryan looked round at the wreckage. "They peck them."

"Peck" wasn't really the word. I wasn't sure how Xathian could have managed to meet the hens, but they were obviously in touch with their "were" sides. As soon as they'd seen us they'd lined up against the far side of the barn, clawing the floor, like bulls pawing the ground. Any minute now they were going to charge.

"If you lay a hen down on its back on a straight line it can't get up," said Ryan. "Their eyes get fixated behind them on the line. Anyway." He rubbed his hands together and bustled over to an old screen. "I've been thinking about your Derrick problem and I think I may have found a way forward."

He emerged from behind the screen again,

holding a large plastic box. "It's an old toolbox. My mum used to keep paints and stuff in it. Look." He swung it open. "There's a big space at the bottom for a larger phobia and you could use all these other compartments for mice and birds. Then the small top ones could have buttons and spiders and suchlike."

"Ri-ight." I peered at the dusty compartments and tried to imagine it. "And when all the . . . phobias are there all together in the box, what happens? Apart from them all eating each other, I mean."

"Or fighting?" suggested Boy Dave.

"Not a problem," said Ryan confidently. "Once the box is closed, the compartments fit on top of each other so the individual segments will be blocked off."

"And let's say we need to open it again?"

"Well, you would get each phobia out one at a time and expose Derrick to it. I mean, seeing as we don't know what his phobia is, the most logical thing would be to expose him to all possible phobias in one hit. He's bound to be terrified of one of them."

We thought about this.

"Like this is a sort of phobia kit," I suggested.

"Exactly." Ryan nodded happily. "It works on the same principle as when they test you for allergies. They expose you to about six or seven on your skin and see which one goes red."

"It's going to be hard getting them all together," I pointed out.

"We're off to a good start, though," said Ryan. "I've got loads of spiders, and tons of mice. And we can snip the buttons off some old clothes."

"What about being phobic to colours?" I asked. "Dulcie terrified a man with a green dress once."

"Well, I've got quite a few white mice," suggested Ryan. "We could paint them."

"Okaaay. How will I know it's the colour he hates and not the mouse?"

He tutted impatiently. "If it's the mice he'll show fear at the sight of all of them. If it's the colour he'll only show fear at that particular one. Then all you need to do is remember which it was." He grinned. "Simple."

I started to feel nervous and excited at the same time. Ryan's plan might just work. Except. . .

"Look, I really don't want to do anything else to upset my mum. She was in tears the other day."

"We know," said Boy Dave. "You said. But who was it that made her cry?"

"Well . . . sort of me."

"But mainly. . .?"

I nodded. "You're right. He's got to go. For her sake and mine. And everyone else's."

"Exactly," said Boy Dave. "And guess what? Great news. Mum made me go into town with her the other

144

day and I saw something interesting. I think I might know where we can get a snake."

OK, this is the bit where in a proper book we would miraculously have found a pet shop owner who miraculously agreed to sell us a snake without a whole load of interrogation. Back in our totally different world full of paranoid adults. . .

"How?" we asked. "Where?"

But Boy Dave grinned annoyingly. "You'll just have to wait and see."

I went home feeling happier than I had in a long time.

It was only when I got there that I realized I'd forgotten something crucial.

Twenty-seven

Mum was in the middle of comforting Joanna about something that had ruined her life again (but at least it wasn't me this time) and Derrick was keeping up a long droning commentary on a cookery programme. By the looks of it Dad was down the pub.

Mum gave me a suspicious look. "You're back late. Rehearsals finished an hour ago."

Oh NO! I could have kicked myself. Of course, we had to time our lives around rehearsals now.

"I . . . was a bit worried about my lines," I explained casually. "So I stayed behind to ask."

Luckily at that moment Derrick's drone got louder. "I wouldn't do it like that myself. No, no."

Mum looked distracted but for some reason the mention of rehearsals made Joanna's despair worse.

"It's not fair!" she wailed. "I mean, I'm, like . . . way better than her at acting."

"Better than who?" I asked. I thought I already knew; I just wanted to see if I was right.

"Collette!" wailed Joanna again. "I would have been perfect as the Virgin Mary and me and Adam would have been amazing together. I mean, Collette's almost as tall as him and she doesn't even like the same music. She hasn't even. . ."

Ha ha – knew it! From the moment I saw Collette and Adam together onstage. . .

"But you're goth now," I told her nicely.

Joanna pierced me with red eyes. "What do you know about *acting*? The whole point is you can be whatever you want. I can be *goth* now and the *Virgin Mary* onstage. You're only an *extra*! You don't even need to be there."

"Well I'm sorry!" I snapped. "Maybe I won't be prancing round trying to be the centre of attention like some people. Except – oh! I forgot – you're not in it, are you? And I have quite a lot of lines actually. I have to say oohh and ahhh in all the exact right places . . . and hallelujah."

Mum, who had looked like she was about to ask a bit more about why I was late back, smiled. "I think it's great that you're taking it so seriously, Jordan."

"I am!" I told her. "I mean, that's why I wanted to go over my lines. I don't want to shout out hallelujah in the wrong place all on my own and make myself look stupid, do I?"

Joanna said. "You always look totally stupid."

"You'll be fine," said Mum kindly. "There's plenty more rehearsals to go, you'll get the hang of it. OH

FOR GOODNESS' SAKE! Derrick!" Throughout all this he'd been keeping up a continuous critical drone about the cookery programme. "Have you *ever* actually cooked anything yourself?"

Derrick gave her a thoughtful look. "Aye, well, back in the days before all these newfangled gadgets and. . ."

I closed off my ears and sighed. There was no point staying up. I was just about to go upstairs when Joanna said, "I'm going upstairs. I just need to, like, be alone right now."

"I think I'll turn in too." Dulcie shot Derrick an irritable look and started to roll up the raggedy scarf she was knitting as a Christmas present.

"Just us," Mum said brightly to me when they'd gone. "Why don't I make us a hot chocolate?"

"That sounds like a very good idea," said Derrick, who could obviously pay attention when it suited him. "I'll have some of those nice oaty biscuits with it if I may."

I followed Mum into the kitchen. Dulcie had been making her non-cook chutney and it stank of vinegar. Everywhere you looked there were jars of hideous brown gunk.

"Make him go," I told her crossly. "He's spoiling everything."

"Jordan." She looked at me tiredly. "How can I tell him that now I know his wife's not dead he is no longer welcome in my house?"

"That sounded quite good – the way you said it just then."

But she pulled the sort of grown-up face that means you don't understand difficult grown-up type stuff and poured the milk into the pan.

I drank mine on the stairs in the hall just so as I wouldn't have to sit in the same room as Derrick again. I must have been tired because I had a sudden dreamlike image of myself in a starry cape on a smoky stage saying in a meaningful voice, "Behold – my magic box of tricks!" And I pulled out a huge long snake that looked a bit like Dulcie's knitting.

Twenty-eight

As it happened, the box was a bit of a problem in so much as it might have been easier to just take Derrick to the zoo. Apart from the mice and spiders, there was difficulty getting hold of all the alive-type phobias.

Ryan had said we could use the werehens as the birds, but given what they'd done to the pagan mushrooms I hated to think what they'd do to someone who tried to cram them into a box.

We had to wait for Thursday night's rehearsal before we could go into town. It was late-night opening, but we still only had an hour to get there. Crow's Ridge is a narrow hilltop that runs the two straightest miles between our village and the town.

Unless there's a good moon it's pitch black after dark on the ridge and we had to jog all the way by torchlight. We came in shivering off the ridge, along a muddy tree-lined lane, and fifteen minutes later we were staring at the contents of a bucket in Mike's Fishmongers.

"Erm. . ." said Ryan doubtfully after a bit. "I kind of see where you're coming from."

"It is a sort of snake," said Boy Dave excitedly. "That's what they call them – sea snakes!"

"Or . . . *eels*," I pointed out. "I mean, being realistic, there are some quite big differences."

"I think," said Ryan, "The main problem is that they're a sort of fish. Not being in water for any length of time will be a problem for them."

"I've thought of that," said Boy Dave proudly. "He only needs to be out of the water long enough for Derrick to see him. After that he can be popped back into his water compartment. He probably won't even notice he's been out."

"You think he could actually be in the box, then?" I asked doubtfully.

"Well that's the brilliant bit! This one can't come out of his water. I mean, even if he wanted to try and escape or eat the others or whatever, he'd be too scared to risk it."

At that moment the man from the fish shop came out from the back.

"Crab sticks?" he asked boredly.

Ryan pointed at the bucket. "Actually we were wondering how much these were?"

The fish man shot a surprised look at the writhing black tangle.

"You can't keep 'em as pets, you know," he said sternly.

"Oh no," said Ryan. "It's just that we're . . . er . . .

doing a school project on fish and . . . erm . . . fish type food. We thought we could use it for show and tell. We'd bring it back afterwards," he offered.

I don't know what it is about grown-ups, but as soon as you tell them you're doing a school project they immediately want to get involved.

Ten minutes later, the fish man was still trying to "help".

"Yes," he carried on enthusiastically, "the Japanese have some amazing aquaculture, huge great pools full of eels – although they like to keep 'em small – more of a delicacy. Now! In this country we tend to jelly 'em, but, being in the countryside, we have a lot of gypsies coming in. Whenever we get a catch I keep a few live ones back. It's one of their traditional meals, you see? I mean they cook 'em first, obviously, but they don't jelly 'em. In fact if you want to know about unusual eating habits you should talk to a few gypsies – hedgehogs!" he said grandly. "Now there's an unusual dish for you. . ."

It seemed important to stop the fish man before he started listing every unusual dish he could think of. After the restaurant I'd had enough of that sort of thing to last a lifetime.

"But you could sell one to us," I suggested. "Even though we're not officially gypsies."

"Yeah," said Boy Dave, "now we've talked to you I think we could do a really good project. With all your help we might even be . . . er . . ." (I should say that even Boy Dave went a bit red at this massive lie) ". . . top of the class."

"Well. . ." The fish man peered doubtfully into the bucket. "I could let you have this little one for a couple of quid."

I checked it out. "That one's a bit too wormy. We really wanted one that looked more like a snake."

"Only because," said Ryan quickly, "some of the class might not believe us."

The fish man ummed and ahhed. "I could let you could have this one for a fiver."

It was curled up underneath the others so it was quite hard to see, but from where I was standing it looked about the same length and thickness as my arm. I was about to say that maybe we should go for a more middling one when Boy Dave said, "Great!"

He was obviously really pleased that his idea was going so well. We handed over the remains of our firework money and the fish man disappeared out back.

He reappeared a few moments later with what looked like a small garden fork with the spikes twisted round on each other. He handed us a large polythene bag full of murky-looking water.

"Hold this open and make sure you don't drop it." He plunged the fork into the bucket. "They slip out of most things so you have to twist 'em up a bit, see?"

He gave a skilful twist of the fork. When he flicked it up again there was a cross-looking eel in the prongs. We jumped as he sploshed it into the bag.

"Mind you pour him into a bucket when you get home," called the fish man as we made off back into the darkness. "Good luck with the project!"

Shivering, we switched on our torches and set off back across the ridge.

I was carrying the bag a little way out to the side of my body and we weren't even halfway across before it got really heavy and uncomfortable. Boy Dave took a turn and on a sudden urge I bent down and shone my torch into it. I stared into the murky water and from its depths two black snaky eyes stared broodily back at me.

Twenty-nine

Mike (after his original owner, Mike of Mike's Fishmongers) settled quite well into his bucket, but Ryan reckoned he wouldn't last too long in the same water. He started researching eels and at the weekend Mike moved house into a new saltwater aquarium. Meanwhile I was wondering how to get Derrick on his own.

It was the last Monday in November and by then we'd had Mike for three days. Dad was just about to leave for work when Mum called into the hall, "Do you want to eat early or late tonight?"

"Why can't it be normal time?" He poked his head back round the door.

"Early sounds best," said Derrick.

"Review meeting at the school?" Mum shot me a look.

"Takeaway," said Dad grimly. "We'll be needing something to cheer us up after that."

On the other side of the breakfast table, Derrick was like a volcano about to erupt.

"And the arrangements for the . . . er . . . rest of

us?" he enquired anxiously.

Dad glared at him. "You know where the kitchen is."

"We'll get a takeaway for everyone," said Mum quickly.

Before Dad could moan about the expense she slid a meaningful look in Derrick's direction and muttered, "We don't want to come home and find a horde of locusts has descended, do we?"

"It's all systems go," I told Boy Dave and Ryan that break time. "Joanna's going out and Mum and Dad will be gone from about six. I can sneak out straight after them."

"Don't worry," said Ryan. His eyes gleamed behind his glasses. "I'll have everything ready and prepared."

I arrived panting and red-faced at Ryan's shortly after six. "I've just run all the way. I thought it would take a bit long to get it all back, so. . ."

"Right," said Ryan in a businesslike way. He had the box all ready in front of him on one of the pagan mushrooms. "I won't open the lid just in case, but the mice are in the middle compartments; you've got red, green, purple and yellow. The others wouldn't fit so I stuck with accident and sickness type colours."

"That's OK," I told him breathlessly. "We probably got a bit carried away with all the different shades anyway."

"They've got loads of cheese so they're happy. Buttons and spiders in the top. I managed to get you a couple of those huge house spiders as well," he said proudly.

"Great."

"And Mike's at the bottom in some of his water."

"Did anyone ever tell you you're brilliant?" I punched his arm.

Ryan tried to look cool about this but you could tell he was secretly a bit pleased. "I'll bring the hens up later."

Boy Dave caught me halfway down the road. He was on his bike. "Phew, sorry I'm late. I got away as soon as I could. I've come to help you carry the box."

"Thanks. It weighs a ton!"

"That's why I brought the bike. We can balance it on the saddle."

When we reached my gate we stopped. For a moment we just stood looking at the box. It seemed so still and normal-looking propped up on the saddle like that – it was hard to imagine all the stuff inside it.

"Right well," said Boy Dave eventually. "Good luck. Hey. . ." He leaned over the gate. "Don't worry. It's bound to be one of them."

"It has to be," I told him grimly.

With a terrible feeling of desperation I searched every room in my house before I had to admit the truth. Derrick wasn't there. Dulcie wasn't even there to ask where he'd gone. I felt a sudden rush of anger. Honestly – the one time I'd actually come home and wanted to find him there!

Gloomily, I wandered into the living room. On the floor beside the settee the large yellow toolbox was eerily quiet. Maybe the air holes hadn't been big enough? Maybe they'd all died. I felt bad just thinking about it.

There was nothing to do but eat one of the sandwiches Mum had left out and wait. I had the TV on but I still jumped at every little sound hoping it was Derrick coming back. The display on the DVD box clicked away the seconds. Seven o'clock, seven fifteen. . . Soon it would be too late. Where could he possibly be? Where was Dulcie? Surely Mum and Dad hadn't taken them to the "review".

I'd never been so glad to see Nemesis in all my life. She came bounding in and licked me happily. Of course, I should have realized; Dulcie had taken her for a walk. Funny time to take her for a walk, though. Dulcie doesn't normally go out in the dark. Seconds later, the reason appeared in the living room doorway.

It was Derrick, wearing one of Dad's scarves and a flat cap.

"We have just been to walk the dog," he told me depressedly. "I wouldn't normally want to walk a dog. They are unhygienic and do their. . ."

"Derrick and I were left here on our own." Dulcie shuffled in behind him. "I was finding it very tedious so I said I would take Nemesis to sample the night air. But Derrick, who obviously didn't want to be left on his own with no one to talk to incessantly, decided to join me. He was most disappointed to find out that there are no food outlets of any kind in the village. Thank you, Derrick dear, I have heard quite enough about your opinions of dogs for one evening! I am now going to get myself a large glass of sherry!" She creaked off haughtily in the direction of the kitchen.

Derrick sat down and gave me a depressed look. "Will the rest of your family be gone long, do you know? Only I was wondering when. . ."

Trying to shut out the drone, I reached down and hoiked the toolbox on to the settee.

"I have some doubts about, particularly, foreign food outlets. They seem to be neither one thing or the other in so much as. . ."

Nervously I unclicked the latch on the box. Derrick started to recite a list of questions you should ask before you bought a takeaway. I lifted the lid an inch or so and peered in through the crack. A couple of sweaty-looking mice scuttled impatiently. Great, they were still alive. I slid my hand through the gap until I felt fur.

"I ask them," continued Derrick, "whether the herbs and spices they use are fresh produce or dried. And whether they blend their own spices at the restaurant or. . ."

I hauled the first mouse out of the box. It wriggled madly.

"LOOK. . ." I said loudly. Holding it by the tail, I waved it in front of Derrick. "It's a –" I did a quick check "– *yellow mouse*."

Derrick stopped mid-sentence. I wouldn't say he shook with terror exactly, but he did look a bit shocked.

"Mice carry disease and fleas," he said after a slight pause. "You must take it outside and hit it with a broom."

"That's a very *large* mouse, Jordan dear!" Dulcie had come back in and was standing by the doorway.

"Isn't it?" I shoved it back in and grabbed the next one. "And look, that mouse was yellow but this one is *red*." I was starting to feel like a children's TV presenter. "Red!" I said again, thrusting it at Derrick. Without warning there was a sudden hideous jabbing crunch and my whole finger dissolved into an agonizing mash of blood and gristle. "ARGGHHH!"

There was no way I could have hung on to it. With a final flash of red the mouse hurled itself suicidally on to the floor and disappeared under the settee.

Through the agony I heard the sound of the front door opening. Quickly! Pain or no pain I'd got this far and there was no way I was giving up now. I grabbed a handful of buttons and threw them at Derrick.

"BUTTONS," I cried. "SPIDERS."

There was a sudden strong smell of Indian takeaway and I looked up to see Mum and Dad with their arms full of small brown bags staring down at me from the doorway.

"Jordan!" Mum stared at Derrick, who was trying to brush all the spiders and buttons off. "What on earth is going. . . OH GOSH – MICE!"

I looked down. Oh no, somehow they'd managed to get all over the settee. Well, no point wasting the opportunity.

"Oh, so there are," I said in a pleased, surprised sort of way. "Look, there's a green one. And a purple one and a. . ."

Derrick, not exactly overcome with terror, lifted his feet as they started to leap off and run around the floor.

"Oh . . . my . . . GOD!" Joanna suddenly appeared behind Mum and Dad in the doorway. Her eyes boggled.

"Are those, like, rats?"

"Large mice," Dulcie told her. "Apparently."

"But, they're, like, all different colours?"

"JORDAN!" yelled Mum. "DON'T JUST SIT THERE!"

"I HAVE TO," I yelled back. "BECAUSE IN MY BOX. . ." With a sudden flashback to my starry cape dream I bravely plunged my bleeding hand into the water. "I have this HUGE SNAKE!"

When you think that there's a well-known saying about eels, it was stupid to be as surprised as I was at what happened next.

Mike wasn't even halfway out before he exploded from my grasp. With a hideous writhing leap he rocketed through the air, uncurling as he went. By the time he hit the floor it was like he'd tripled in length and become a demented elephant's trunk thrashing about on the carpet. Derrick screamed and went pale, but then so did everyone else.

"JORDAN!" Mum, who had dropped her bags at the sight, was obviously trying not to become hysterical. "DOMINIC! DO SOMETHING."

Dad, who seemed suddenly to have come back to life, dropped his bags as well and lunged at Mike in a sort of rugby tackle. Mike leaped out of his way under the kitchen table and Nemesis, who had been hiding under there, shot out barking and cannoned into Derrick, who'd been trying to leave.

"I don't think that will work," I told Dad. "You

need a sort of special fork."

Derrick, who was all off balance, stepped backwards into a bag of Indian takeaway. It stuck to his foot like a weird brown boot. He tried to hop into the hall but bumped into Ryan, who was on his way in.

"Oops, sorry," said Ryan, waving a basket in at him. "Hope you don't mind, but the door was open. I've just popped round to show Jordan my hens."

Thirty

"It took me almost the whole evening to try and explain," I told the others gloomily. It was lunchtime, and it being the first of December, we'd popped up to see Mr Jolly setting up his decorations. "I had to sit on the bed in Mum and Dad's bedroom as well so Derrick couldn't hear. It was really embarrassing. Then they made me stay up half the night trying to catch the mice. I hardly got a wink of sleep. And Mike's absolutely exhausted."

"Did you get them?" asked Boy Dave.

"No, of course not. I've told them we can borrow Ryan's trap but they're not in the least bit grateful. They just don't seem to be able to understand that I was doing it for everyone."

By now we were trudging back up the steps for afternoon lessons.

"It must have been hard to punish you for it, though," said Boy Dave. "Seeing as they've used up all the punishments already."

"Well, now you come to mention it, that is quite strange because, unless you count trying to get the mice back, they didn't actually mention punishments at all."

We were on our way past the lockers and a sudden loud bang made us jump.

"Sorry," said a familiar creepy voice. "Did I startle you?"

Xathian was a few lockers up. It was like he'd been hiding behind the locker door that he'd just slammed shut. We suddenly realized that a few of the other bat boys had appeared from the shadows and were lounging around eyeing us moodily. We tried to ignore them and walk past, but Xathian jumped in front of us.

"Where's Jo?" he demanded.

Jo? Oh!

"You mean Joanna?"

"Yes, she likes to be called Jo now. She's not here today and she's not returning my texts."

It was quite funny to see him all jumpy. It's hard to say this about such a pale person, but, for him, he looked a bit flushed. I felt a grin spreading across my face.

"We-ell . . . she's off sick with a cold, I think." Xathian tried not to look relieved. Ha ha, now for the slam dunk. "But you know, she doesn't fancy you any more."

There was a bit of a rustle among the other bat boys. Xathian's face went through a load of changes in about two seconds – total surprise and disbelief, tight and twitchy, a few more, ending in a not-very-good attempt at casual.

"I love her as a friend," he said grandly. A couple of the bat boys giggled and he went even pinker under his paleness. "I just . . . noticed she wasn't around, that's all. I care about her, you know? I care for all my. . ."

"Brethren?" suggested Ryan.

"Nest?" I suggested.

"You've got competition, mate," grinned Boy Dave. "It's seventeen and a bit more muscly."

"Ignore the little squirt!" Louse gave us his best up-and-down look. "Girls don't like beefcakes anyway."

"Yikes!" said Boy Dave. "It's the bald terror."

"Yarroo," said Ryan. "Let's scarper."

"Yeah," I agreed. "Before we get stampeded by girls all thirsting for his wimpiness."

By now Xathian, who obviously had never had a sense of humour and wasn't about to start getting one now, had gone almost red.

"Who?" he demanded. *"Who?"*

But we were on our way into class and Jefferson was waiting. Not even a hardened creature of the night like Xathian would risk bursting into the lair of a lunatic.

*

That night it was rehearsals. We passed Mr Jolly's to see it all lit up and then went to check on the ice rink. The way the weather had been going it could freeze over any day now. But despite a great evening, after I'd said goodbye to Boy Dave at Hangman's Lane I felt a wave of gloom wash over me.

It had been one thing going home when there was hope of getting rid of Derrick, but now it was like walking into torture, especially with all the new stuff for him to drone on about.

Almost as soon as I got in Mum said she wanted a "quiet word". By now this was code for "in the hall". Something about the way her arms were folded made me twitchy.

"Where were you tonight?" she asked in a voice that was way too calm.

"Rehearsals." I tried to sound casual. "Why?"

She nodded grimly. "Rehearsals."

"Uh huh."

"No you weren't."

"Yes I . . . was."

"Don't lie to me, Jordan. Joanna was there."

Joanna!

"No she wasn't, she's ill."

"She does have a nasty cold, but tonight was the only time she could audition."

My head was whirling. Audition? Joanna? So all

our winding up Xathian had actually been true. Joanna just couldn't bear the thought of Collette getting close to Adam. She was going to try and be in the show – maybe even just as an extra – to spoil Collette's chances.

I thought quickly. "I never saw her."

"No," said Mum tiredly. "You wouldn't have done, on account of the fact that rehearsals were cancelled because they were auditioning for the new Mary. Joanna told me when she got back. She says there were only about five of them there. So, I'll ask you again. Where have you been?"

And that was that. The end.

When I told Boy Dave the news the next day he went pale.

"There is one way," I said, trying just for a second to put my own gloom behind me. "You'll have to show up at the beginning and end of rehearsals from now on. That way Joanna will vouch for you. She got the part of Mary, by the way," I added even more gloomily. "Apparently Collette's broken her ankle."

"Your sister probably shoved her down the stairs," said Boy Dave bitterly. "Collette's lucky she's not bound and gagged in the boot of a car somewhere."

That Thursday, Mum made me help her and Dulcie fix up the Christmas shoeboxes. They do them every year, for poor kids overseas, so they can have a

Christmas present. As I sat at the kitchen table filling box after box with pens and sweets, small dolls and toy cars, I tried to think of those kids and not feel sorry for myself, but it was hard.

It was like a massive dark mist creeping into me. Bitter thoughts turned over and over in my head – no one had asked me if Derrick could come and stay. It wasn't my fault that Xathian had come barging into our fireworks display and the fireworks had been dodgy. And OK, so I wasn't going to rehearsals, but I hadn't been doing anything bad. I wasn't going to do anything bad again; I'd already made up my mind not to for Mum's sake. As for the whole phobias thing – well it was my house too! Why shouldn't I get rid of Derrick? It wasn't as if anyone actually wanted him there.

I suddenly realized that the mist was really a slow, building anger. I was like something captured that had writhed and screamed and fought and finally, when there was no hope left, given up. I remembered back to Mike, that first night on Crow's Ridge, when I'd shone my torch into the bag and seen his black eyes in the murky water. The look he'd given me then – it was how I felt inside: trapped in murky darkness with nothing to do but brood on the downfall of my enemies.

That night I couldn't sleep. Joanna was sniffling and snoring in her sleep. Every now and then she would half wake up, blow her nose and throw her tissue at me. If only I could have my room back again. Or my life. There had to be a way. I couldn't just give up. I'd never had a bad Christmas and I wasn't about to have one now. But what could I do? Everything I'd tried had gone wrong. And I seriously couldn't afford to get into any more trouble.

Gloomily I flicked a sticky tissue off my pillow. Yuck, no wonder I wasn't feeling very well, with all those germs gunking up my pillow. It was disgusting the way she slung them about! It was . . . well it was. . . It had been Derrick's word I was looking for, but before I had time to finish the thought another one shoved it out the way.

I threw back the covers and padded over to the window. Slowly I pulled back the curtains. By now the same things were turning over and over in my head – Derrick, food, germs, Christmas, food, germs.

Leaving the curtains open I flopped back on to my bed, where I could watch the moon. There were tissues all over the floor, like little crumpled white birds in the moonlight, but instead of being disgusted, I stared at them interestedly.

It had been so obvious I hadn't seen it at all. But it had been there – hanging as thin as a spider's thread in front of me. And now, finally, I could see it for what it was. . . One last tiny chance.

Thirty-one

That first week of December the atmosphere at home was terrible. I mean there was Derrick terrible and then there was Joanna. She was almost managing to outdo Derrick when it came to talking. And no prizes for guessing what it was about this time – the nativity.

"And, like, Adam the butcher's boy was there? And we just had this amazing chemistry. And Harold Thorpe Jackson, the famous producer, just held out his hands and said I *was* Mary and. . ."

Joanna's hair was still black, but even that was fading. As far as Joanna was concerned Harold wasn't the only one who thought she *was* the Virgin Mary. Joanna did too.

Luckily, in a way, what with the early dark nights, Dulcie was finding it harder to take Nemesis for her evening walk, so Mum agreed to let me take over. I was only allowed out for forty-five minutes, but at least it meant a bit of peace and quiet. Nemesis and I took to wandering around the silent village looking at the lights. More often than not we would end up at the village green. While Nemesis woke up the ducks, I would sit on the bench by the pond. On quiet nights I could hear the rehearsals going on up the track in the village hall.

Boy Dave and Ryan came to meet me when they could, but I felt bad asking them to come just for half an hour or so. I suppose I was waiting for the right time to tell them my idea, but in a way it was like they'd done enough. Instead I spent my time by the pond plotting on my own. It was the only thing that kept me going.

That weekend the temperature outside dropped to freezing.

Boy Dave and Ryan tried to be tactful but they could hardly hide their excitement.

"Does it work, then?" I asked gloomily on Monday morning. There had been a rehearsal that Sunday so I knew they'd tried the ice rink out. They looked at each other.

"It's great!" Boy Dave burst out. "You can hardly stand up on it."

"Oh. Well that's brilliant."

There was a moment's guilty silence while they both looked at different things.

"It's not the same without you there," said Boy Dave nicely. He sounded like he meant it. "Look, surely there must be some way you can get free for a couple of hours?"

I shook my head sadly.

"We can go during school," said Ryan. This was quite a big thing for him because he really likes lessons and hardly ever bunks off.

Me and Boy Dave looked at each other, remembering the terrible parent-teacher meeting.

"Just once," said Boy Dave. "And then we'll be really good until the end of term. After all, we might never get another chance."

"Just once," I agreed. "To see what it's like."

The thought of doing something exciting for the first time in days had filled me with a kind of sudden crazy energy. As we headed off into the woods I felt like a polar bear bursting from its crate and bounding out across the frozen planes. Talking of freedom: "What about Mike?" I asked suddenly. "Have you let him go yet?"

Ryan pulled a face. "There's a bit of a problem. With him being a sea eel, he might die if we put him back in the river."

"And if we take him back to the fish man," said Boy Dave, "he'll be eaten."

"Oh!" I hadn't thought about this. When we first got Mike it hadn't seemed so bad that he would be eaten in the end; a bit revolting, yes, but not exactly tragic. Now, though, in a strange eely sort of way, he'd become our friend. After all, it wasn't his fault he had normal slippery eel type instincts, and when the time had come he'd done his best. The least we could do was to try to do our best for him.

As I thought this, my heart sank. Normally getting to the seaside isn't a problem for us – it's only a half hour bus ride. But for me at that moment, it might as well have been another planet.

"When are you going to take him?" I asked sadly.

Boy Dave looked at the ground. "Probably on Saturday rehearsal."

"We thought we'd plop him off the end of the pier," said Ryan. "We were going to do it off one of the breakwaters, but we wanted to give him a good chance to swim out – you know."

I imagined Mike's last triumphant leap to freedom. It would be amazing to see him hit the waves. He'd probably given up hope of ever swimming in the sea again.

"Well . . . say goodbye from me," I said sadly.

Once we'd climbed over the wall to the ice rink, though, whatever sad thoughts I'd been having completely – I was going to say evaporated, but skidded away is better.

I stared out across the thick, white layer of ice. I could hardly believe it was real. I mean, all we'd really done was stick a pathetic trickling hose into the pool. And it had turned into this brilliant,

brilliant winter activity. Our very own private ice rink.

That feeling lasted until I actually tried to go on it. It was like the Mike experience all over again – you expect it to be slippery, but not that slippery. One minute I was like a hamster running on a wheel and then, at the same time (and when you describe this it doesn't seem possible), my legs spread out in completely opposite directions.

At the pool edge, Boy Dave and Ryan doubled over with laughter.

"We were like that!" said Boy Dave.

I tried to swallow down the gagging-type pain you get from falling over really hard on your bottom.

"Observe and learn, oh apprentice." Boy Dave lowered himself over the edge. With a push he propelled himself off one end of the pool, and with knees bent and arms out, he slid a length at a great speed to the other side.

"You can do a width," he explained. "But you crash into the other side really hard."

"There isn't time to lose any momentum," explained Ryan boringly.

I did start off with widths, though.

Icy air is the best air there is – when you've been breathing it in for a while you feel clean inside and really happy. Out there on the ice that day, it was impossible to worry about anything.

Gradually, I fell over less and less and then suddenly it was like something just clicked into place. It must only have taken a few seconds until I reached the other side, but just at that moment it felt like ages – like I was sliding along, perfectly balanced, for miles and miles.

"What did you think of it, then?" asked Boy Dave as we reluctantly headed back to school for end-of-the-day register. There was no other way to say it, and even this wasn't good enough.

"I loved it!"

He and Ryan grinned.

Ryan said, "It's our best activity ever." His glasses had frozen patches that glittered in the light. For him it must have been like looking at the woods through ice.

"It was a great idea," I told him generously.

Unusually for him, Ryan tried to look modest. "Well, I couldn't have done it without your help. Anyway, wait till you see my invention, you're going to love that too!" Oh well; modesty does have its limits. "All I need now is a compressor."

"What's that?"

"It's a sort of powerful blower. It might be used to blow something out, but basically it blows air."

There was silence while me and Boy Dave tried to imagine the invention.

"You're not actually going to try and blow us into outer space, are you?" I asked nervously.

"Of course not." Ryan looked scornful. This might have been reassuring if he hadn't followed it with, "It would take a lot more than a compressor to do that. Your dads have got one," he added casually. "I saw it the other day in the alley."

Me and Boy Dave looked at each other.

"Oh no," said Boy Dave. "There is just no way."

"Just a thought," said Ryan cagily. "You know, tossing a few ideas around."

Thirty-two

The next day was Saturday and I could hear the rain hammering on the window. The ice rink wouldn't last long in this and it was Mike's last day. I sighed; I would have liked to be able to see him off. Still, at least Joanna was already up. Which was strange when I came to think of it. I normally get up first.

I pulled back the curtains. The sky outside was dustbin grey and Crow's Ridge had almost disappeared in the sleet. Normally in the morning I wonder what to do that day but there was no point now. I banged my fist against the window in frustration – if only there was some way I could put my plan into action. There was a tap on my door.

Mum was wearing a skirt and shirt with a pair of smart shoes. When she kissed me, she smelled of perfume. "Good morning, sweetheart, sleep well?"

"Where are you going?" I asked surprised.

"We're taking Dulcie up to London," she said brightly. "'Proper' Christmas shopping."

I grinned. Dulcie had been angling for this for ages

and she normally gets what she wants in the end. I'd assumed by "we", Mum had meant her and Joanna. Normally Dad would rather set his feet in concrete to get out of it, but. . .

"Your dad and me are going to manage Dulcie while Joanna goes off and does her own thing," said Mum.

While she'd been saying this, Mum had automatically taken me out some clothes and was folding them out ready at the end of my bed.

"Why don't you come with us?" she asked kindly. "It would be nice to do something as a family for once."

Actually it would have been quite nice without Derrick for a change, but the soaring feeling of fantasticness was like one of Ryan's fireworks going off inside me.

"I . . . maybe another time," I told her feebly. "I'm feeling a bit woozy. I expect I'm coming down with Joanna's thing."

Mum felt my forehead. "You feel OK. Maybe you're just sickening." She tucked me back in bed. "I'll tell Derrick he's not to disturb you. There's a steak and kidney pie in the fridge that you'll have to share for lunch." She poked her head back round the bedroom door. "And don't go out in this wet. Your dad can walk Nemesis when he gets home."

I grinned to myself. I had every intention of going

out in the wet. Soaked to the skin in brilliant, brilliant rain.

As soon as they were gone, I hid in the bathroom and rang Boy Dave. I chose the bathroom because I had a paranoid idea that, with no one to talk to, Derrick might come and find me.

"I can come," I almost yelled. "I can come and see Mike off."

There was a bit of a silence at the other end.

"Er . . . well . . . we had decided to put it off for today, actually."

"But why? Mike would love all the rain."

"Yes, but think about it. We'd either have to walk him back across the ridge and get a train, or we'd have to wait for a bus for hours, and either way we'd have to lug him all the way to the pier. And I'm actually a bit sniffly already," he added plaintively.

It felt selfish to point out that this might be my last chance to come with them. Also, I'd just realized something. For all my plotting by the village pond there had been one big rock-like problem that, apart from in daydreams, I hadn't really been able to get past. Now, though, by the most brilliant twist of fate, it was gone. All the way to London, in fact.

Half an hour later, I ducked sneakily into Boy Dave's den for a secret meeting with him and Ryan.

*

Derrick was watching the TV when I got in.

"Your mother said we were to have the pie for our lunch," he said resentfully.

I got the feeling he'd been waiting for me. I wouldn't have minded, but it was only twelve-thirty.

"That's right, I'm just going to put it on." I rubbed my hands together cheerfully. "It's our special Christmas pie, so I can hardly wait."

Derrick looked a bit interested. "Oh aye? I must say, I've never heard of a Christmas pie before. Unless one counts mince pies, of course, which I find are so often—"

"We don't ever have those," I interrupted. "So I wouldn't know. Still, better get on."

Before he had a chance to say anything else, I disappeared into the kitchen.

The first thing me and Boy Dave did was heat the real pie-filling up in the microwave and eat it. Then we got down to work.

"I hope you don't mind," I told Derrick. I was laying the table and trying to remember where you put the things. "But a friend of mine's going to join us. He loves my mum's special Christmas food, so I said it would be OK."

Derrick looked anxious. "Will there be enough to go round? I think the pie was really only meant for the two of us."

"Don't worry." I made a big thing of placing a bottle of soya sauce so Derrick saw it. "We'll make sure you get the lion's share."

Boy Dave and Derrick sat down at the table.

"This is Boy Dave," I told Derrick. "He's Big Dave's son. Big Dave works with my dad."

Derrick looked at Boy Dave boredly. "Aye, well," he began. "I daresay builders. . ."

Back in the kitchen, I grinned to myself. Boy Dave was getting seriously droned at. Trying not to breathe in through my nose, I looked down at our handiwork. Derrick had almost half a pie and we had the tiniest slices we thought we could get away with. There were sliced carrots as well, but we hadn't bothered to cook them, just sprinkled them with parsley.

Derrick sniffed at his plate. He looked a bit like I must have done in the restaurant.

"Mum's special Christmas pie," I told him. "And herby carrots. Tuck in, we gave you biggest bit."

Derrick turned his slice on its side. The glistening contents oozed out thickly.

"I love it," said Boy Dave. "They have it every year. I always beg them to save me a slice. It's why I was invited round today. So I could have some specially, actually before Christmas Day. By Boxing Day it's normally all gone, you see," he added inventively.

"Soya sauce?" I offered.

Derrick looked at me disapprovingly. "One should

never season a dish without first trying the taste."

He suddenly realized he'd backed himself into a corner. His eyes slid from one to the other of us. We were watching him expectantly. Reluctantly he sliced a careful piece of pie and raised it dripping to his mouth.

"Urghh!" He spat it out. "Sorry, I . . . just wasn't expecting it to be cold."

"We always have it cold," I told him. "And Mum does normally like people to have nice manners. Especially on Christmas Day."

"Mmm." Boy Dave had just popped a large piece into his mouth. "Can't beat it." He'd made sure it was all pastry, but it was still pretty daring.

"Yes, yes, of course," said Derrick embarrassedly. Bravely, with me and Boy Dave watching, he cut another piece.

"The," spluttered Derrick, through his next mouthful, "tanginess. What is that?"

"Could be the vinegar?" I shrugged. "Or maybe the. . ." I picked mine around a bit. "Erm . . . little green bits that look like frog's skin?"

Derrick's jowls wobbled. "And . . . what ingredients exactly does your mother use to make the . . . er . . . pie?" He tried to make it sound casual but it came out sort of gagging.

"Well, it's mainly Dulcie that makes it," I told him. "Didn't you see all the jars?"

Behind his little gold glasses, Derrick's eyes popped. Even he couldn't have missed all the non-cook chutney everywhere.

"The . . . stuff in the jars goes into the pie?" he said faintly.

"That's why she makes so much of it," I explained. "So we can make lots of spare ones and eat them all in the run-up to Christmas."

"Great, isn't it?" said Boy Dave enthusiastically. He nodded across at me. "You only ever have it with carrots, don't you? So as not to spoil the flavour."

"I mean, personally," I told Derrick confidingly, "I'd like to have a few more things to go with it. And I really wish we were allowed Christmas cake and Christmas pudding and cream and all that stuff, but Mum's very strict." I had a sudden burst of inspiration. "She makes sure all the things we would have been having get put in the poor children's shoeboxes."

Derrick put down his knife and fork and looked at me in the same way my dad looks at parking tickets. "And this is all your family has to eat on Christmas Day?"

Me and Boy Dave laughed.

"Of course not," I told him cheerfully. "We have a main dish as well."

A look of something that wasn't quite relief spread over Derrick's face.

"Ahh," I said. There was a knock on the door. "This will probably be it now."

Derrick watched apprehensively as Ryan staggered in and plonked a bucket on the table.

"I did try to interest them in my hens," he explained. "You might remember? I came round the other day. But they insisted on sticking to their usual."

"Thanks for looking after him." I said. "We were a bit worried after I accidentally let him escape that time."

Derrick heaved himself out of his chair and leant across the table. As he edged towards the bucket his apprehensive look turned into dismay, then something like horror. Deep in his gloomy depths Mike flicked his body bad-temperedly and turned a single evil black eye upwards to meet his gaze.

"We like them cooked the gypsy way," I explained.

Thirty-three

That afternoon we caught the bus into Brighton. By then we felt it was the least we could do.

The pier was almost empty and those few people who were on it were too windswept and wet to give three boys struggling along with a bucket a second glance. Our heads were down against the wind and through the gaps in the boards, we could see the sea smashing angrily against the pier legs far below.

"I don't know if he's going to make it," Ryan shouted. His glasses were streaming with rain and his hair was plastered flat. We'd given up on our hoods and hats. They blew off the second we tried to put them on. "What if the wind takes him?"

Me and Boy Dave didn't reply.

We were almost at the end now. Ahead of us stretched the angry sea, and far, far off on the horizon was a single bright patch of light.

As we leaned on the rail looking at the churning sea, I think we all knew that this was Mike's last chance. He wouldn't survive much longer in Ryan's makeshift aquarium and there was no way of knowing when we'd get another chance to bring him – or if the wind here on the seafront would even drop again before the summer.

Ryan had been right, though; Mike was a big, strong, heavy eel but he would be nothing against a wind like this. Chances were he'd be thrown back and smashed against the side before he even hit the waves. I gazed down at him sadly.

"You're going to have to take your chances, mate."

"OK," said Boy Dave abruptly. "Let's do it."

With solemn faces, we picked up the bucket and prepared to pour Mike over the side. He was almost gone when I pulled the bucket back again.

"Wait! Drop it with him. The heaviness of the water might be enough to take him down."

Normally we wouldn't throw things into the sea. But the way I saw it, Mike belonged there. And if he was ever going to have a chance of making it out to that tiny bit of sunlight on the horizon, the bucket was more or less his only hope.

There was no way we could throw them clear, so we dropped the bucket like an anchor. The water flew out as it went, but it was enough. Like a jerky torpedo it plummeted down and crashed into the waves.

We leaned as far over the edge as we dared. Way down below we could just make out a small black shape still curled up at the bottom. The bucket bobbed wildly, first flying dangerously towards the pier legs, then away again with Mike still curled up tight inside.

Then came a huge wave. Rising high like a shying horse it smashed down and the bucket disappeared completely.

When, many long seconds later, it bobbed back up again, Mike was gone.

Thirty-four

That evening a confused conversation took place. Mum had started to have a go about the state of the kitchen but when I told her I had cooked the pie for Derrick, she stopped.

"Honestly!" she said crossly. "That man! He's so lazy."

"That's OK," I told her cheerfully. "I didn't mind helping out."

She gave me a suspicious look, but I suppose she couldn't think of anything to be suspicious about.

The confused conversation happened a bit later over tea. Dulcie had been going on about certain shops "selling out to the masses" and Joanna had been arguing that the shops in London were "amazing" when Derrick, who had been unusually quiet, stared abruptly down at his mashed potato.

"Mashed potato is pleasant enough," he began. Mum sighed; we'd had the mashed potato being "pleasant enough" conversation a few times. He let out a great jowl-wobbling sigh.

"Jordan tells me that you normally have your

Auntie Dulcie's . . . erm, jar filling pie on Christmas Day?"

Mum and Dad, who had got used to drowning him out, looked slightly surprised.

"Sorry?" said Mum politely.

"He was saying about Auntie Dulcie's special . . . er . . . filling Christmas chutney," I chipped in quickly. "Uncle Derrick tried some today and really liked it. He was really glad to hear we'd be having it on Christmas Day as well."

Mum and Dad looked even more surprised, but Dulcie said in a pleased sort of way, "He certainly shall!"

It was probably the first time in her life she'd ever been pleased with Derrick.

"And he enjoyed the carrots with the pie as well," I ploughed on. "I told him we always had those on Christmas Day as well, don't we, Mum?"

"I. . ." Mum looked a bit dazed. "Yes, of course."

By now Derrick's face had fallen by about a mile. "And all the Christmas pies and puddings are donated to charity?" he asked dolefully. "Instead of—"

"I was telling Uncle Derrick about the shoeboxes," I interrupted. "And about how you try to give all the good things of Christmas to the poor children."

"Well, yes," Mum was looking completely confused. "If anyone deserves it, they do."

My heart upped a few beats as I saw an unmistakable "about to mention the eel" look on Derrick's face.

He had already opened his mouth when I said loudly, "I told Derrick all about cooking eels the gypsy way and he seemed quite interested. And, of course, gypsies have a traditional dish of hedgehog as well, but we don't do that. Although maybe we should? It might make an interesting change." I stopped breathlessly. "What do you think? We could try hedgehog this Christmas instead?"

There was silence while everyone looked at me as if I'd gone mad. Then Dad said, "We'll have what we always have, thank you, son." He looked at Mum. "Maybe all this staying in isn't such a good idea after all. You need some fresh air, mate," he said to me.

"Sorry," I said sadly. "Was I rambling again? I've caught myself doing that lately. Perhaps it is all the lack of fresh air . . . and exercise and that. I'm just so excited about Christmas dinner, that's all."

I risked a peep at Derrick across the table. He was staring straight ahead through his little glasses and shovelling mashed potato into his mouth as if starvation was staring him in the face. I suppose from his point of view, it was.

That night I could hear what sounded like Derrick pacing the floor in Joanna's old bedroom. After about half an hour the pacing stopped and there was a loud thump on the floor. I'd heard that sound once before – out in the hall when Derrick arrived. It was the thump of a suitcase all packed and ready to go.

Thirty-five

The next day Derrick told Mum and Dad he would be staying at the Old Manor Hotel.

"I feel it's only fair," he told Dad solemnly. "And I will probably be more comfortable there. It's not as if I'm going far. I will still be able to visit often enough, between the hours of ten and twelve and three and five."

Dad had been looking amazed since Derrick broke the news that morning.

"Ten and twelve," he echoed. "Two and five. . . Oh, right." He'd obviously just worked it out. "Well . . . erm . . . we're sorry to see you go," he said with grown-up hypocriticalness. "But," he added quickly, "it's probably for the best. I'm sure you're right, the hotel will be a lot more comfortable."

Mum and Joanna kissed Derrick's jowly cheeks, which made him go a bit pink and pleased-looking, and Dulcie gave him a couple of jars of home-made non-cook chutney.

As the sound of his taxi pulled away we all – and

all at the same time – leant against the nearest wall. For a few seconds we just stayed there like that enjoying the silence, then Dad looked at the door and muttered, "And a lot more expensive in all, mate! Right, let's 'ave it."

I was surprised to find my whole family looking at me.

"I'm sorry, am I missing something?"

"OK," said Dad tiredly. "What did you do to him?"

"I'm sorry, Mum." I looked at the floor uncomfortably. We were all sitting round in the living room with me not enjoying being the centre of attention. "I didn't tell you before because I didn't want to upset you. It's just the lunch we had yesterday, I think there was something . . . well . . . a bit off about it?"

Mum frowned. "What do you mean, a bit off?"

"I don't know. It tasted fine to us . . . *me*. But, well, I really hoped you'd never have to know this, but Derrick actually spat his out."

"Jordan. . ." said Dad warningly.

"It's true! He spat it out. It was disgusting. Then he asked what was in it so I tried to think but couldn't remember. And after that he refused to eat any more."

Mum looked confusedly at Dad. "There's nothing wrong with the freezer, is there?"

Dad was looking at me through narrow eyes. "No."

"And I haven't been sick or anything," I said helpfully.

"No," said Dad again.

Joanna said, "Maybe it was like because Jordan made the pie Derrick was just terrified of all the germs?"

Cheek! But without knowing it she'd played right into my hands. I did a face a bit like Dulcie's "remembering" one.

"I suppose my hands might have been a *bit* dirty. I mean, I'm sure I washed them but, you know, with Derrick pestering me to get lunch ready. . ."

Later that Sunday Dad had a "word" with me. Something along the lines of, "Blah blah blah any more trouble blah blah me to answer to blah blah you need to show you can be trusted blah etc."

The good bit is what he said next: "So I'm going to let you go out with your mates again on one condition: that you tell me and your mum where you are going, what you are doing and that you are in by eight every night, you got that?"

"It's normally nine," I reminded him. "And that was three conditions."

Dad gave me a look. "Don't push it, son."

"Yes," I mumbled. "I mean, no." My legs were

jiggling like they were trying to run out of the door on their own.

"And another thing," Dad called after me. "The first whisper of trouble and you are nailed to this spot until the next millennium. *That* is a promise!"

Thirty-six

The great news was that once my dad had said I could go out, Boy Dave's dad said he could as well, so he didn't have to pretend to go to rehearsals any more. To make things even better, it was the last week of term.

By Tuesday, I was in the best mood ever. The air was so cold my breath was like clouds and it was ten more days until Christmas without Derrick. There was still a bit of a problem about money. After paying for Mike, and even after searching the field on our hands and knees, me, Boy Dave and Ryan still only had about ten pounds each. Still, a lot could happen in ten days, and I had the definite feeling that, having spent so long on a bad downhill bit, we were going to go uphill again like a rocket.

Boy Dave must have felt the same because that morning when we met at the end of Hangman's Lane, he greeted me with a huge grin.

"Brilliant, isn't it? My dad couldn't even get the key in the lock of his van this morning it had iced up so badly."

It was icy all right. All along our road that morning people had been rushing bad-temperedly around their cars with kettles of water and scrapers.

Unfortunately it hadn't quite been bad enough to close the school.

"I want you all to write a small essay on your best winter memory," said Miss Lovejoy that morning in English. "It could be about. . ."

I faded her out and stared longingly out of the window. Me, Boy Dave and Ryan had a best winter memory all right, and one that we'd rather have been doing for real right then.

"My best winter memory," read Emma Chichester. "We went to Winter Wonderland. There were real-life reindeer and a Santa with a sleigh. And he took us round on the sleigh and the bells jingled. . ."

"And there was a Santa's grotto," said Poppy Lockhart, "where you could see all the toys being made, and we had real-life reindeer too and it was all snowy."

"Nintendo," read Connor.

Lin Maize's was a bit better. Lin has black eyes that are spookily like Mike's, and a particular way of staring at you. "I prepared the duck," she said coldly. "I was the one who broke its legs."

Straight after school, me, Boy Dave and Ryan bolted for the woods. By the time we crawled out of the ice rink for a breather, night was falling fast.

"We knew you'd be here." Claire did what she always does and jumped right off the top of the wall instead of hanging first like a normal person. She can do it backwards with a somersault too in daylight. "What are you doing just sitting? By the way, this is for you." She handed something to Ryan. In the dark it looked like a scrap of paper, but when he held it up to the moon we saw it was a twenty-pound note.

"We should have given it to you sooner," explained Daisy. "But there were some issues with us hanging out with you for a while."

"That's half." Claire lowered herself into the pool. "We thought it was the least we could do after. . ."

She and Daisy burst out laughing.

"After all the black smoke," finished Daisy. "By the way, what's that? I never noticed it before."

It was like a really tall, thin triangle-shaped scaffold with what looked like a huge glowing star on top.

"Looks like a Christmas decoration." Ryan shrugged. "It's probably something to do with the hotel."

"Makes up for the stingy lights on their tree," I said.

Claire and Daisy's ice-skating was better than my first attempt but still hilarious. Shame it was so dark, but we didn't dare use torches. The last thing we wanted was someone from the hotel coming to investigate. It was the longest we'd ever managed to last at something like this without getting caught.

Talking of the hotel, I could have sworn I saw an enormous, mournful Derrick-like teardrop shape passing the window on its way down the stairs.

Thirty-seven

We were warming up in Boy Dave's den when Ryan said, "How much do you think people would pay to have a go on real snow?"

"Nothing." I clicked open a can of fizzy orange. "On account of it falls from the sky and goes everywhere."

"But what if it doesn't?" persisted Ryan. "Fall from the sky, I mean. And you could sell it anyway?"

"You mean, like, bag it?" asked Claire. "It's a good idea, but you'd never be able to store enough to make it worthwhile."

"No, no, you don't understand! I mean make it! Like so it's not snowing anywhere else, but if you pay to go into, I dunno, a winter extravaganza. . ."

"If I was you, I'd find another way of putting that," Daisy told him. "*Extravaganza* has a whole new meaning these days."

Ryan ignored her. "So that even if it wasn't snowing anywhere else, you could do all the great stuff like snowball fights and tobogganing. And with an ice rink to go with it, how much do you think people would pay?"

"Loads," said Boy Dave. "But it's never going to happen round here, so there's no point really thinking about it."

"That's just where you're wrong!" Ryan's eyes gleamed behind his glasses. "My new invention," he announced proudly, "is a snow machine!"

There was a stunned silence.

"Are you sure?" I asked doubtfully. "I mean, if you can make snow, you can make rain. And I happen to know –," I was proud of this knowledgeable bit "– that some of the world's greatest scientists have been trying to make rain for years."

Ryan looked at me a bit interestedly. "Well, you're right, of course. But actually you're missing the point. You have to have rain – or precipitation – in order to make snow, or in our case, a water hose and an air compressor, but after that it's fairly simple. They do it all the time at ski resorts. I was going to have it just for us, but then in English today I got thinking. Why don't we have our very own Winter Wonderland? You heard them all today; they love those sorts of things."

"It's a great idea," I told him, though I was still finding it hard to believe that he really could make snow. "But are you sure something bad wouldn't happen? You know how things are right now."

"There is one thing," said Claire. "If you do it by

the ice rink, the people from the hotel will be out like a rocket."

"But the ice rink is a great attraction," said Ryan.

"There's five of us," Daisy pointed out. "And no one's ever come out before. The hotel's right over the other side of the car park, and if we sell tickets, we could control the numbers."

"True." Boy Dave nodded. "And we could make the tickets all official-looking – like it was the same as the circus coming – call it Mr Snowy's Winter Wonderland or something."

In the end we decided that Mr Snowy sounded too made up. The final tickets had a photograph of a smiling, welcoming-looking man who we named as the new improved Uncle Derrick.

Jolly Derrick's Winter Wonderland Experience comes to town. For real snow and ice sliding along with all the joys of winter. Follow the signs from Hangman's Lane.

The "joys of winter" were proving to be a bit of a problem, though. It had been hard enough getting hold of a snake, never mind reindeer. We wondered about dogs with stuck-on antlers, but we only really knew two dogs and they were crazy. And people might think it was a bit weird.

The next evening we found Mr Jolly standing in his garden. He was staring anxiously up at his roof to where a snowman was teetering on the edge.

"Your new stuff looks great," I told him nicely.

Mr Jolly's front garden was now filled to bursting with a huge inflatable sleigh and six monster reindeer with dozy-looking eyes.

"Arrived two days ago," said Mr Jolly, looking at it worriedly. "Bit late, but got it all up in time for the grandchilds at least."

"How many grandchildren have you got again?" Ryan asked nicely.

Mr Jolly thought about this.

"A great many of them," he said finally. "Is all I can tell you."

Ryan stared thoughtfully up at the teetering snowman. "Actually, there was something we wanted to ask you."

"Be the Santa and give out all the presents?" said Mr Jolly eagerly, when Ryan had finished.

"Ye-es. But we . . . I mean the organizers . . . are a bit short of a sleigh. I don't suppose there's any chance, I mean if you helped, that you could bring along some of your Christmas things? There's already an ice rink and a snow machine, but it needs something really Christmassy."

A strange look spread over Mr Jolly's face.

"A *snow* machine!" His eyes shone. "A *snow*

machine!" he whispered again.

"It belongs to the organizers," said Ryan. "But . . ." You could see the sinister cogs of his twisted brain churning ". . . I'm sure they would let you borrow it – for the whole of Christmas Day if you liked. Maybe even a bit longer, you know, in exchange for you being kind and helping out with the Winter Wonderland."

"That's very generous," breathed Mr Jolly. He rubbed his knobbly old hands together and repeated the deal back to himself. "I'm to be the Santa, with my sleigh. And then I shall have the machine for Christmas Day and maybe a few days after that!"

I was starting to feel a bit guilty. He was so *pleased*. It would be terrible if he was disappointed. On the other hand he'd been really gutted about the nativity and at least this way he got to take part in a Christmas-type activity.

"I shall go in and phone the grandchilds," he announced, bustling off up the path. "Tell them my good news."

He was halfway through his front door when he turned back. "I expect you'll all be my elves," he said wisely. "To help give out the presents."

"Ye-es," we said slowly.

Later that evening, we made a big batch of washing-up liquid bubble bath with bottles from the recycling bins. There weren't any lids but Ryan had managed to persuade Andy from The Black Horse to give him a load of corks, and for colour we'd used a few dollops of food dye. Instead of a "Jolly Derrick" on the labels there was a smiling child with "Bubblefun Bath" printed in swirly letters. All they needed now was a bit of tinsel round the necks to finish them off.

"They actually look quite good." Boy Dave sounded surprised. "I mean you could almost sell them."

Ryan's mum's barn looked like a magician's den full of coloured potions.

"Seriously, though," said Boy Dave as we wrapped them up in bits of a roll of old red wallpaper, "we could actually start up a shop."

"We could make bath bombs too," said Ryan. "That's just Epsom salts. And we could melt down old bits of soap to make new bars – with maybe a little splash of perfume."

I should say at this point that the last thing me, Boy Dave and Ryan had ever seen ourselves doing was opening a sort of beauty shop, but by the time we'd finished wrapping that evening we were even discussing the best way to make body cream.

There was just one teeny snag. The Winter Wonderland was due to take place that Saturday and by Friday lunchtime we still hadn't sold a single ticket.

"I don't understand," moaned Boy Dave. "In class that day they were all mad for it."

"Uh-oh!" I interrupted him. "Troop move out." I thought this was quite funny.

We'd managed to keep out of Xathian's way, but now we had a new person to try and avoid – well we always did avoid her but at this time of year it was worse. Poppy's birthday was right after Christmas. We'd managed to swerve her party last year but she was desperate for Boy Dave to come to this one.

"Hiya." Poppy tried to make it sound casual. She and Emma were wearing tinsel in their hair and looked completely stupid (but what's new?).

"How's it going?" said Emma shyly. Her nose had gone really red in the cold.

"For the last time, Ploppy," began Boy Dave rudely. "We do not want to come to your stup—"

But I'd just had a sudden thought. "Actually," I interrupted him. "You're just the people we wanted to see."

Poppy and Emma goggled.

"Yeah," I carried on nicely. "You remember those brilliant essays you wrote about your nice outing to Winter Wonderland?" Boy Dave stifled a groan. "Well, we were just saying, I mean I know you're having a great party of your own and obviously we'd love to come, but maybe you could help us out with something as well?"

After school finally broke up that day (YAY!) me and Boy Dave caught up with Poppy and Emma.

"You did say we could keep twenty pence for each one we sold," said Poppy nervously.

"Yes, yes, of course," said Boy Dave impatiently. "How many did you do?"

Poppy and Emma made a big thing of each getting their leftover tickets out.

"Are you going to be at this . . ." Emma peered at the front of the ticket. ". . . Winter Wonderland experience then, David?"

Poppy pretended to be counting money like she'd never put her up to it.

"Yes," sighed Boy Dave. "I'll be there."

"And we're really looking forward to your party," I told Poppy nicely. "Now, come on, how much did you make?"

"Seventeen!" I told Ryan cheerfully when we found him in the schoolyard. "And Poppy reckons some of her friends are going to come along and pay on the day as well."

Boy Dave looked grumpy. "It's not going to be much fun with them all giggling around when we're trying to have snowball fights."

"I dunno," I grinned. "I wouldn't mind seeing them on the ice rink. And I know she sold a few to Connor and Cal. If we get the snowballs ready first, they won't know what's hit them."

"Just so long as she never sold any to Slime-ian," said Boy Dave, who seemed determined not to cheer up. "He'll probably try and turn it into a gig."

We were about to head off when Ryan said, "Er. . ." He was acting a bit nervous. "I've forgotten something. Look, if I don't catch you up I'll meet you at the ice rink at eleven tomorrow, OK?"

We stared. "But it's the last day of term!"

"Well, I . . . it's the snow machine and things," He shuffled awkwardly. "I have to get them ready."

I suppose we should have seen it coming, but right then we were too busy looking forward to celebrating in Boy Dave's garage – days and days ahead with no school and Christmas in a week. I guess we just weren't in a suspicious frame of mind.

Thirty-eight

The next day I was woken up by excitement. It was a brilliant day – cold, but not freezing, with a low-down, bright winter sun. The Winter Wonderland wasn't due to start until two but by the time me and Boy Dave arrived at eleven-thirty, Ryan was already there.

"It doesn't look like I'd imagined," I told him. I was trying not to sound disappointed. Ryan's snow machine looked like a home-made, not very good, robot.

"The hose goes in this metal bit at the back," explained Ryan. "And the compressor plugs in here."

"You got hold of one then?" said Boy Dave cheerfully.

"Er, yes. Then the extension lead from the changing rooms is here, so we plug it in and. . ."

Ryan flicked a switch. A noise like a loud hoover echoed across the courtyard.

"I haven't attached the hose yet," said Ryan over the racket. "But it's pretty cool, isn't it?"

I shot a nervous glance in the direction of the hotel. With any luck they'd think it was woodcutters.

Me and Boy Dave left Ryan fiddling about with his machine and went to open the gate. There wasn't really any reason why the people coming to Winter Wonderland couldn't jump the wall like we did, but we figured that the new improved Jolly Derrick would probably have an actual entrance.

It was one of those old wrought-iron gates, with swirls; dark gold with rust and covered in ivy. We'd been thinking we could just break the lock, but when we turned the old handle it swung open at first push.

"That's weird," Boy Dave frowned. "You'd think they'd have kept it locked."

"It probably rusted away." I laughed. "And there was us jumping the wall all the time." I was dragging the pool tarpaulin across the courtyard. "Give us a hand. We can stick it over one of the stable roofs so people don't keep tripping over it."

By now, Ryan had managed to get the snow machine to the point where it was making slush.

"I think it's the attachments," he muttered as I climbed up the side of one of the stables. "The problem was I had to sort of guess which ones to use."

"It's still good," I told him. "Perhaps it just needs to warm up."

I was secretly pretty doubtful about whether it would ever work, but I hoped it would. Particularly for Mr Jolly.

It was about twelve-thirty when me and Boy Dave went to collect him. He was waiting patiently by his gate dressed in a full Santa outfit. He'd even stuffed a cushion up his robe to make him look tubby.

"Best Santa clothes they had," he told us. Behind the white curls of his false beard his weather-beaten face was glowing with pride. "Don't know why I never thought of it before!"

"Yes," agreed Boy Dave kindly as we took either end of his deflated larger than life-sized reindeer. "There you were buying all those Santas without realizing that you could actually be one yourself."

Mr Jolly chuckled. "All that time! But now. . ." He swept his hands proudly down his new fat tummy. "Well. . .!"

"You look great," I told him. I remembered what Harold had said to Joanna about being the virgin Mary. "You *are* Santa!"

"I know," said Mr Jolly solemnly. "And just wait till you see your matching elves outfits."

My trouble, which was getting worse by the minute, was that the happier Mr Jolly seemed to be, the more nervous I felt. At the time we'd asked him to be Santa he'd been a mostly miserable, worried old bloke, with a lot of Christmas decorations. But now it was like his biggest dream come true. By the time we got back to the ice rink I was praying nothing would go wrong.

"It's working!" yelled Ryan as soon as he saw us. "I've finally . . . wow. . ." He tried not to laugh.

Me and Boy Dave shuffled embarrassedly and tried to avoid jingling the bells on our hats too much. Mr Jolly had seemed so disappointed when we'd tried to get out of wearing the elves outfits that we hadn't wanted to refuse.

"Best they had," Mr Jolly told him proudly. "Don't worry, there's one each. Only you'll have to have the red jerkin because there were only two in the green."

"Fab," said Ryan worryingly.

I could hardly believe his snow machine, though. It was standing proudly in the middle of the courtyard spitting out real white, fluffy snow. I mean, it was pretty thin on the ground, but it was still brilliant.

"He he!" Mr Jolly went and held his mittens out underneath. "Would you look at that! And not a drop in the sky."

Actually, as it turned out there was quite a lot in the sky. About a quarter of an hour before the Winter Wonderland was due to open, the first few flakes began to drift down and within half an hour it was almost a blizzard. I would have felt sorry for Ryan but we were all in the middle of a snowball fight and he didn't seem to mind too much. It was me, Boy Dave, Ryan, Daisy and Claire on one team versus Connor, Cal, Steven Longacre, Lin Maize and a few others.

It was brilliant – the best snowball fight of our whole lives. The ice rink was sort of a no-man's-land in between sides and me and Boy Dave, who'd had a lot more practice at sliding, kept jumping in and whizzing across like a bombing raid. Connor and Cal tried a couple of times to do the same to us, but fell over and got hammered.

I think Poppy and her friends tried to slide for a bit as well, but they got in the way of the snowballs and I think they must have gone home.

It was getting on for dusk when Boy Dave said suddenly, "I could eat a horse."

"So could I," said Claire.

I suddenly realized I was starving too.

A few moments later I wandered across the courtyard to Santa's grotto. Mr Jolly was smoking his pipe happily, watching the snow. Everything, for as far as we could see was covered in a thick white layer. He'd gone to stand where he could look out across the hotel car park to the Christmas card woods and hills beyond.

"This," he told me, "is the. . ." He struggled to find

the words. "It's like proper Christmas, isn't it?"

"We're sending out a supplies party," I told him. "Would you like something to eat or drink?"

"Well. . ." Mr Jolly considered. "It should really be mince pies and sherry, shouldn't it?"

Boy Dave and Daisy lived nearest so they set off on a food raid while the rest of us mucked in building a snow ramp. Mr Jolly had been right – it really was like proper Christmas. Even Connor was all pink-faced and cheerful.

On the other hand I couldn't remember being so hungry in all my life.

"Where are they?" Claire came and stood next to me, shivering. "It's going to be really dark soon."

I was about to say that it hadn't really been that long when Daisy and Boy Dave burst through the gate. Boy Dave doubled up, gasping for breath.

"People," he wheezed. He shoved a carrier bag at me. "People. . ."

"They're all coming," panted Daisy. "Through the woods."

"You're kidding!"

"No, seriously." Boy Dave straightened up and stared at the gate. "They must have heard about the wonderland."

Ryan followed his gaze. "How many do you think?"

"Fifty? It could be more."

I blinked. Fifty people. That was . . . there was no time to work it out. Grabbing the carrier bag I ran back through the thick snow, over to where Mr Jolly had just settled back in his stable.

"Look." I plonked a box of mince pies and a bottle of orangeade down beside him. Already the car park of the hotel was filling up with headlights. "Here are some rations to keep you going. You must eat them as fast as you can. There's. . ."

I was distracted by the sudden murmur of many voices. It was like one of Derrick's germ descriptions. People were pouring through the gate and spreading out, by the second. I just stood there with my mouth hanging open, but Mr Jolly took it in his stride.

"Don't worry," he told me confidently. "Santa's on standby, ready to go."

Thirty-nine

Feeling as if I was in a dream, I wandered back to where the others had set up a sort of makeshift ticket barrier. As I arrived a member of the village hall committee stuck his hand in his pocket and handed Ryan three pounds without so much as blinking.

One after the other, adults that I recognized from the village filed in. To my mind most of them were a bit old for our activities, but they all seemed really enthusiastic.

"This *is* an adventure," said Mrs Cooter from the Women's Institute. Mrs Cooter is really thin and gnarled, like a human twig.

"Indeed," said her witchy companion, taking off her mittens so she could open her purse. "A real pilgrimage, following the star of wonder." She pointed at the hotel's tall star Christmas decoration. "Apparently this is to be a modern-day interpretation of the nativity."

"And I hear its producer had something in the West End," said Mrs Cooter excitedly.

I was a bit too busy to take much notice then, but it didn't stop there.

"What time does it start?" asked Mr Elwith, a particularly bad-tempered, Welsh member of the village hall committee.

"Well," I nodded over, "it's been going all afternoon. Ice rink's over there and you can collect your gift from. . ."

"I meant the nativityyyy," bawled Mr Elwith. "What time does the show start?"

I blinked at him. Why did they all keep going on about the nativity and shows? It had said "Winter Wonderland" quite clearly on the bit of cardboard we'd stuck to the tree.

"Er . . . soon," I said vaguely. "Look, Santa's over there. Why not grab yourself some Bubblefun Bath?"

I slid over to where Ryan was happily chinking money into our box. "You haven't arranged a show without telling us, have you?"

"No, but look." He pointed at the box. "This is great, we're quids in."

We were interrupted by a sudden wave of excitement as the dark figures, who had all been wandering round the wonderland, started whispering and pointing towards the car park.

A group of people were making their way slowly across it from the direction of the hotel. They were carrying lanterns on sticks and flaming torches. Behind them were trooping a small crowd. My nerves must have been on edge because I jumped about ten feet as a black mitten landed on my shoulder. It was Mr Jolly.

"My sleigh!" he said, pointing. "One minute I was handing out the gifts and when I looked back again, there it was . . . just *shrivelling* away."

What with one thing and another, it seemed about the right time to grab the money box and head for the shadows of the stables.

"I think someone must have tripped over the leads in the snow." Ryan crouched beside the deflated sleigh like a doctor with a sick patient. "They've yanked them all out. Don't worry," he told Mr Jolly, who was hovering anxiously over his shoulder. "We'll just plug them back in."

But by now the group from the hotel had reached the courtyard. In the lead was a small gremlin-like figure – Harold.

"Excellent," he was saying excitedly. "Progress slowly and . . . solemnly. There's no hurry, let them wait for us."

I stared. I mean you had to hand it to him – this was genius. Harold had somehow managed to lure loads of people out to the dark, deserted stables. The rest of his nest were probably hanging upside down from trees in the dark woods. When Harold gave the signal they would swoop and. . . My heart beat faster.

"Now," said Harold grandly. "Take your place on the podium. Ah!"

He stared at Mr Jolly, who gave him a Santa-like wave.

"This is part of the *set*!" Harold hissed crossly. "You'll have to move."

Mr Jolly, who had been about to hand him a present, looked confused.

There were flaming torches burning all round the edge of the stables now and it was easier to see. Joanna was leaning lovingly against Adam the butcher's boy and clinging to a Mr Jolly style cushion that was stuffed up her jumper.

Even though the situation was pretty dire, I couldn't help cracking a grin at what I saw next.

"Look." I nudged Boy Dave.

"Hang on a minute," muttered Ryan from beside the sleigh. "Right. That's got it."

He stood up stiffly and I pointed to where Xathian was leading a donkey into the stable. "Creep Face has got a new member for his gang."

Boy Dave grinned. "Nah, that's the new singer in his band."

But we weren't grinning for long. Claire and Daisy were worriedly weaving towards us.

"What's going on?" asked Daisy, pointing at Harold.

But Claire was looking up at the stable roof. "Is it my imagination or did that roof just move?"

"OK, everyone." Harold's voice echoed across the courtyard. "Places." (Pause.) "And BEGIN."

Forty

We stared at where Claire had pointed. She was right. The whole stable roof seemed to be sliding towards us.

When me and Boy Dave had slung the tarpaulin over it, we hadn't known it was going to get about a foot of snow on it. And even if it had, in the ordinary way it wouldn't have mattered, except that now. . .

"Oh wow," I goggled. "The whole thing's slipping."

"It must be the fire from the torches," said Ryan. "It's melting the snow."

There was a hideous scraping sound and with lightning speed the whole tarpaulin slid off, burying Harold, Joanna, Adam and the audience nearby in a kind of mini avalanche.

I didn't see what happened next because I suddenly realized that Boy Dave was yanking madly at my sleeve.

"Mrjollyssleighlooksabitfunny." He sounded panicky.

I turned to look. The larger than life-sized sleigh and reindeer weren't larger than life any more. They were gargantuan.

"They're blowing up like a balloon!" gasped Daisy.

The previously dozy reindeer boggled terrifiedly at us from hideously bulging eyes and we boggled back. The whole thing seemed to be doubling in size every second.

"What's wrong with it?" I choked.

"I think it must be plugged into your dads' compressor by mistake." Ryan was on his knees, fumbling frantically in the snow. "It's going to explode unless. . ."

Me and Boy Dave stared at each other. Our dads' . . . WHAT? There wasn't time to think about it, though.

Suddenly and for no apparent reason, the snow machine sprung to life. *Gugugugugug*, it chugged loudly.

A snow-covered person who might have been Harold appeared suddenly in front of us.

"Stop this at once! I am completely unused to such. . ." He caught sight of the reindeer. "Interruptions," he finished faintly.

At that moment the snow machine coughed loudly and spewed a mouthful of slush at him.

Mr Jolly appeared, looking a bit breathless. "I've

just been and switched on the. . ." He saw his sleigh. "Oh my word!"

"Don't worry." I tried to sound reassuring, but it came out a bit distracted. A sort of herd of yetis had raised themselves up from the snow and were stomping towards us through the slush spray.

"Got it!" Ryan scrambled to his feet with a cable in his hand. "The air leads must have been mixed . . . oh." He caught sight of the stomping people.

We would have made a run for it then, except for a sudden evil-sounding hiss behind us. We whirled round and, just in time, threw ourselves on the ground. With a gargantuan shudder, Mr Jolly's larger than life-sized sleigh and reindeer had leapt into the air. We stared up amazed as, like someone letting go of a huge balloon, they zoomed over our heads and rocketed joyfully into the night sky.

As the sleigh passed over the courtyard there was a loud gasp and everything stopped. The whole crowd stood with their heads tipped back, watching in wonder. I suppose some of them must have thought it was the real thing.

If they did, they were just about to experience every child's worst nightmare.

As the last bits of air shot out of the sleigh it spiralled madly upwards like a whirlwind: round and round, up and up. . .

In the darkness, you couldn't see the scaffold that

was holding up the star of wonder – just the star itself, shining, but the sleigh must have gone into it. There was a massive loud crackle and a huge flash of blue lightning, followed quickly by a deafening BOOOOM. Then nothing but terrible silence.

The death of Santa.

Donner, Blitzen, Dasher, Rudolph and the rest drifted quietly down through the moonlight in a thousand tiny fragments.

Just before we slid off into the shadows, we realized there had been a small but meaningful change in the landscape. Not only had the star of wonder disappeared but all the lights in the hotel windows had gone out as well.

Forty-one

"I'm really sorry about your things," I told Mr Jolly. It had seemed wrong to leave him on his own trying to explain it all.

All six of us were tramping through the woods on the outskirts of the village. It was dark and freezing cold and we had no idea where to go, except that it couldn't be home. PC White was bound to track us down eventually, but we figured that if we left it a while they might all calm down a bit.

"Well." Mr Jolly chomped thoughtfully on a mince pie that he'd magicked out of his Santa robe. "It was a spectacle all right." To our surprise, he chuckled. "Imagine that. Never thought it could really fly, did we?"

We exchanged guilty glances.

There was a whole lot that could have been said, but by now we'd reached the edge of the trees. Across a small patch of grass, at the bottom of a snow -covered bank, was the main road. And what we saw down there was like the end of the world.

*

It was as if the entire human race had been wiped out. Absolutely silent, bumper to bumper for as far as we could see, were cars. They were all in complete darkness and some were covered in snow.

For a long while all six of us just stood there looking down. We were scared to say anything. If we did we would have to think about what might have happened. Then Claire whispered, "Look."

Further down on the bank and a little way along was a small group of people. They were standing quite still, listlessly watching the road. Without thinking about it we started to run towards them.

"Oi," shouted Daisy. "What's happened?"

A large man with a blanket wrapped round him turned and started up the bank towards us. As he got nearer we could see he was shivering.

"It's the snow," he called. "No one can move."

Claire stared down at the silent cars. "But where are all the people?"

The large man looked at her strangely. "In their cars. Where else?"

"They must be freezing," said Mr Jolly.

There was silence while we stared down, shocked, at the dead-looking cars.

"No one knows," said Ryan quietly.

"Oh, they know all right." By now the large man had been joined by a smaller one. He was huddled down into his coat. "But nothing can get through. The roads are jammed solid."

"He means the village," I explained. "They've all been out at . . . something. They won't have heard the news."

"Right," said Claire suddenly. "What we're going to do is this. Me and Jordan are the fastest runners. We'll go back and tell everyone. You others get anyone with children and lead them up to the hotel."

"Hotel?" The large man looked surprised. "I never saw a hotel."

"Oh! Well that's probably because the lights aren't working," said Boy Dave a bit guiltily. "But it is there. It's about ten minutes' walk."

"And tell the others we're bringing as much help as we can," yelled Claire as she scrambled up the bank.

Minutes later we were hurtling after our torch beams through the trees.

"Head for the high street," Claire called over her shoulder. "We can bang on the doors as we go."

I sometimes look back on that night and wonder something important. I wonder why it never even occurred to us that people might not agree to help.

They did, though. Before we'd even got the top of the road, doors were slamming and people were trickling out with blankets and bags of food. There was no way anyone could drive but a few were dragging loaded-up sledges and bits of wood.

"Dad," I yelled into my phone. By the sound of it, he and Big Dave were down The Black Horse. "I know, it was an accident. But I can't talk about that right now. There's been an emergency."

By the time me and Claire burst through the door of The Black Horse it was buzzing with activity. I was so cold the hot air made me feel sick. Shirl, the landlady, tried to give me and Claire soup and make us sit by the fire but there wasn't time.

"Boy Dave and the others are taking people with children up to the hotel," I gasped. "But the rest will be stuck in their cars all night."

Big Dave loomed over us. "The boy's still down on the road?" he asked worriedly.

"Yes, but he's fine he's just. . ."

But Big Dave was already gone.

As the night wore on, things got a bit less chaotic. We helped drag sleigh after sleigh of supplies down to the frozen cars and gradually my dad and the others managed to get bonfires lit all along the bank. Meanwhile Jefferson marched up and down organizing everything. After a bit people were even managing to cook jacket potatoes and beans.

It didn't seem to have been that long but it was actually about one in the morning before me and Boy

Dave saw each other again. I was dragging yet another sledge along the main street when he caught me up.

"Hey, you look whacked."

He took the rope with me and we trudged on together. I'd been feeling a bit blurry for ages and the lights from the torches ahead were merging like a kaleidoscope. Still, at least Dad had made me go home and change clothes so I didn't look like an elf any more. And it was only the bottoms of my trousers that were wet now.

"How did it go at the hotel?" I asked.

"They weren't going to let them in at first," said Boy Dave. "Can you believe that? They said it would disturb the paying guests. But then my dad turned up with a few other blokes and kind of shamed them into it. To be fair I don't think the hotel really understood how it was at first. They've got the fire going in the restaurant now and all the tables and chairs are stacked up to make room on the floor. The last time I looked it all seemed quite jolly."

"Just so long as they don't start trying to feed them," I said tiredly. "That'll soon wipe the smiles off their faces."

"Actually," Boy Dave grinned, "they were having some quite nice-looking sandwiches when I left."

There were people everywhere and we hadn't been paying much attention to what was going on, but I gradually became aware of someone calling my name.

"Jordan! *Jordan!*"

I looked up to see Joanna running towards me. She was wearing a huge borrowed coat and woolly hat.

"Quickly." She looked about as tired as I felt. "It's Dulcie."

Me and Boy Dave ran after her. On a grass verge some way down Dulcie was lying completely still on the ground. As my torch beam bobbed across her I stopped. And it was as if my heart had stopped too. Freezing in the snow around Dulcie's head was a large pool of blood.

I threw myself down beside her and tried not to be scared. With her personality hidden away behind closed eyes she seemed to be so papery white and old. And sort of . . . endangered. No, I tried to be honest with myself, she looked dead.

"What was she doing out?" My voice sounded weirdly normal. "She shouldn't have been out in this."

"I don't know." Joanna looked close to tears. "One minute she was coming up the hill towards me waving that bag." She pointed at a carrier bag on the ground. Out of it were spilling piles of neatly wrapped sandwiches and a flask. "And then. . ." Joanna swallowed. ". . . it was like she just flew over backwards."

Slowly I bent my head over Dulcie's mouth.

"It's OK," said Joanna shakily. "She's still breathing. But we have to do something. You'll have to help me get her to. . ."

"NO!" An in-charge-sounding voice above us made us jump. "You mustn't move her." The face was in shadow above his torch, but there was no mistaking the flapping coat and bald head. Louse. "She might have broken her neck or back." He bent down beside us. "If you move her you could do more damage."

"How do you know?" Boy Dave glared at him.

For a second Louse became more like himself. "Because I do, maggot. I learned first aid in the boy scou. . . Because I just do, all right?"

"But she'll freeze," said Joanna desperately. She stood up and stared helplessly at the other people on the street as they trudged past with their heads down. They hadn't noticed us at all. "I don't know who to phone. An ambulance will never get through. I've tried Mum and Dad, but it went over to answer both times . . . and. . ." She gave in to crying. Not her usual dramatic, still-trying-to-look-pretty type crying, but real quiet sniffly tears.

She was right about the cold. When I'd touched Dulcie's coat, it had already been wet through.

"Hey," came a creepy voice behind us. "Don't worry, Jo."

We might have known, wherever Louse was. . .

Xathian went to put his arm round her, but then he sort of froze.

"OH GROSS!" He stared down at Dulcie and his eyes went wide. "Is that . . . blood?"

Me and Boy Dave, who had ripped off our coats and covered Dulcie over, stared at him in disgust.

"We have to get one under her head," said Louse. "Mine's an army coat; it's not soft but it's really waterproof. It'll be better keeping her covered on top." He looked up at Xathian. "It'll have to be yours."

Xathian stared back, horrified. "But there's . . . it's . . . I mean . . . she's . . . Look, this coat cost eighty quid. . ."

"Here." Joanna ripped hers off. "Have mine." She stood above us, shivering in her "Mary" dress.

There was a bit of a silence; then Louse reached out and took it.

"Gently," he said, turning back to Dulcie. "Don't jerk her head. Dig out the snow a bit instead."

Joanna's phone went. "I don't know," she was saying. "She's bleeding from her head but we can't tell. I know. We have. Yes. OK." She sniffed loudly. "OK." She turned back to us. "They've called the vet. He's coming with a tractor."

I don't care what they say about our village emergency services, they rock.

*

233

Actually, even though he wasn't a human doctor, the vet was great. By the time he arrived, Dulcie had started groaning and was sort of starting to come round.

"I won't give her anything in case they have to operate," he said. "Ray Chiggley thinks we can get her across the hills in the tractor. Once he hits the town the roads are better. They may be able to send an ambulance out to meet us."

Our dads, the vet and Mum (who'd come flying up the hill at a hundred miles an hour) managed to get Dulcie lying on a board and then into the tractor. Meanwhile me, Joanna, Boy Dave and Louse huddled shivering by the engine, trying to stay warm. Xathian had skulked off into the darkness – like anyone cared.

With a thump and a shudder, the huge wheels of the tractor ground the snow, spraying it wide. Ray Chiggley made a neat end of field type turn and the next thing, the lights of the tractor were disappearing slowly up the hill, with Mum, Dulcie and the vet inside.

"Right." Our dads (who'd come flying *down* the hill at a hundred miles an hour with a load of other blokes) looked down at us. "Bed!"

Which surprised Louse a bit, because it seemed to include him. As it happened, he slept on our couch, and I think he and Joanna might have nicked some of

Dulcie's brown yuck to drink.

Boy Dave had Joanna's bed and she had the one in Derrick's room, which was really hers if you think about it. If we hadn't been so tired it would have been weird. It was years since me and Boy Dave had been allowed a sleepover. I think we talked a bit and drank hot chocolate made in the microwave, which tasted better than anything I've ever had since, but after that, well. . .

The next thing I remember is Dad stomping into the bedroom.

Forty-two

I knew Dulcie must be OK because when I asked Dad he called her an old bat. Apparently she had a broken wrist and they were keeping her in because of the bang on the head but that was all.

"Not that a bang on the head would change her much," said Dad. "I hope your mother's told them she's already got birds in the attic." But I could tell he was secretly glad she was all right.

Me and Boy Dave were trudging after Dad and Nemesis (who was loving rolling on her back in the snow) up the road. "We've none of us got any food left in our houses," Dad explained, grinning, "so the hotel's going to try and sort out breakfast from their freezers."

At that moment, me and Boy Dave both got texts from Ryan.

"Been up all night! At hotel having breakfast," he said. "WhereRU?"

"2mins," I texted back.

It was like nothing you'd recognize. There were people all over the floor and children running around. Ryan was there with a bacon sandwich and his hair and glasses all messy.

"It's mad!" he said. "By the way, I think we've finally found your uncle's worst nightmare."

Sitting mournfully on his own in a corner of the restaurant was Derrick. He was chewing depressedly on a single piece of toast and was the only person actually sitting at a table.

"There's no food to speak of," he droned when he saw us. "I haven't had so much as a wink of sleep and now we have a situation where. . ."

"It'll be back to normal soon," I told him comfortingly. "And I bet they do a great Christmas dinner."

It seemed important to try and cheer him up a bit. The last thing we wanted was him turning up on the doorstep again. I needn't have worried.

Me and Dad had just got our sausages rolled in bread when Joanna turned up. And she wasn't alone. With her was a small, dumpy woman in a pink coat and an old-fashioned hat.

"She, like, just arrived?" Joanna hissed to Dad. "I didn't want to be on my own with her. She's, like, completely crazy – like she wants to kill someone?"

The woman had been glaring round the restaurant evilly, but now her ratty little eyes fixed on Derrick. Not even seeming to have noticed us, she stomped across the floor towards him – slinging children out of the way as she went.

"What's all this!" she bellowed. "I have just flown *all* the way from *basking* in the sun on board a luxury liner because *you* were meant to be at death's door and look at you! Sitting there! *Gobbling* away as if there was *nothing* wrong with you while I have been in a *freezing* cold taxi *stranded* in the middle of nowhere with a *big* hairy man who smelled of *CHIPS!*"

Derrick looked like he'd seen a ghost. In a way I suppose he had.

"But Maureen." He stared up at her miserably. "I never . . . I mean, I'm staying here for my Christmas. Of course there's nothing wrong with me, I never—"

"Well that's *not* what I heard!" interrupted the person who I had guessed was poor Aunty Thing. "I received an *urgent* message saying you'd been *rushed* to hospital and I must come home immed. . ." She stopped. Slowly she turned around until her ratty little eyes met my dad's.

He winked at her and raised his cup of tea. Out of the corner of his mouth he said, "You should have more faith in me, son."

Forty-three

There are a few more bits to this story. The snow thawed that day, and by mid-morning everyone was finally on their way. But they didn't forget. Not knowing anyone's addresses, they all sent Christmas cards and pretend medals and suchlike to The Black Horse. There were boxes and boxes of them.

As soon as the traffic got going the TV people came and called us a "village of heroes". Most of us were catching up on our sleep but obviously Joanna hauled herself out of bed for the occasion. By the time she'd seen herself over and over again on national television she'd completely forgotten about the nativity stuff.

As for the Winter Wonderland, the hotel seemed pretty much to have forgotten about it all. If anything I think they blamed Harold, because it was his star that caused all the problems. But they were booked solid for weeks, so they were pretty OK with it all.

By the time we all went back to school, everyone had normal-coloured hair again and it went back to being the normal goths who were there before Xathian, and who got on with their own thing without trying to convert everyone else. Even Xathian started to look a bit more normal (really dorky actually). I hadn't realized that he had a mum as well, but she came to pick him up once and got chatting to my mum. Apparently Harold's "something big in the West End" was called *Minxie and Her Muffet Pals*, and was a travelling show for the under-fives.

I guess they couldn't really have been vampires – not with a show called that.

As for Mr Jolly, he had the snow machine right up until when our dads started work again and we had to sneak the compressor back. He also had a brand new larger than life-sized sleigh and reindeer, paid for with our gate money. Funnily enough, no one ever did ask for it back. I suppose they forgot – either that or they thought Harold had run off with it. This time, though, Mr Jolly had perky, alert-looking reindeer who would know a great big bit of scaffold when they saw one.

He also set up his own "hire a Santa" business and by spring he'd branched out into "hire an Easter bunny" as well. He even calls himself Mr Jolly now, although once his grandchilds had all gone home again he looked more like Mr Exhausted.

We didn't go to Poppy's birthday party in the end. Her mum said we weren't welcome because Poppy and all her friends were dyed different colours and the whole thing had been very upsetting. Mind you, they weren't alone. By the time everyone had had a go of their Bubblefun Bath, most of the village was muticoloured.

And last but not least, we never did see Mike the eel again. But then we never really expected to.

Dinah spent her childhood immersed in 'boy' books such as the Just William series. She was inspired to write the WARNING! books after working as a youth worker in rural villages and many of her characters are based on people she met along the way. She even "borrowed" the name of her husband's joinery firm (Rise Joinery) to use as Jordan's dad's business, not knowing at the time how successful the books would become! Dinah lives in East Sussex with her husband and two children.

If you liked this, look out for more hilarious adventures by Dinah Capparucci

WARNING!

THESE BOOKS CONTAIN MADNESS
AND CAUSE UNSTOPPABLE LAUGHTER!

To begin with, I should say that
none of this was our fault.

When a reality TV show came to our
school, NO WAY were me, Boy Dave and Ryan
taking part! We were too busy trying to stop an
alien invasion. If we'd realized the monstrous
TV presenter wanted to invade our minds, we'd
probably have made a run for it sooner.

We didn't know things would end in
total disaster. . .

When the new kid sucked Boy Dave into a crazy computer-obsessed world and made him a gaming zombie, we knew we had to do something. Me and Ryan just wanted to remind him the real world was fun.

We didn't know everything around us would get annihilated. . .